# GLASS BOTTOM

# GLASS BOTTOM

*A Novel*

SONALI PRASAD

PICADOR INDIA

First published 2024 by Picador India
an imprint of Pan Macmillan Publishing India Private Limited
707 Kailash Building
26 K. G. Marg, New Delhi 110001
www.panmacmillan.co.in

Pan Macmillan, The Smithson, 6 Briset Street, Farringdon, London EC1M 5NR
Associated companies throughout the world
www.panmacmillan.com

ISBN 978-81-19300-98-3



1 3 5 7 9 8 6 4 2



Typeset in EB Garamond Pro by R. Ajith Kumar, New Delhi
Printed and bound in India by Thomson Press India Ltd.

*For my mother, father and sister*

*Something in the air wants us too much.*

—ILYA KAMINSKY

# I

# 1

*TO THE WOMAN BEFORE SPRING:*

*This we can sell; we have always sold similarities. In place of an insect tongue, a fishing line enters the throat of an eager white flower, down, down, twisting, till it breaks the anther and releases the pollen grains.*

*All's well suited to the tanks.*

# 2

GUL'S BRAID WAS THE LONGEST it had ever been. It had been long in her youth, reaching to her waist when she stood, but not to the extent that she could curl up in bed, catch it between her thighs and bring it beyond the navel. The hair making a hairpin. The length so just but kind. She generally wore it coiled around her neck, and everywhere she went—to the beach, campus, market—people looked at her and touched their own hair: slyly patting their buns, smoothing their tresses, tapping the bare spot near the forehead. There was envy, adoration and dread, and Gul didn't mind—such was living under the gaze of long, bright candlesticks hanging by their wicks, each wick wont to curl in its own flame—until she encountered those who looked relieved. They altered her step, the few who refused the prowl of the finger, confident of having just enough on their heads to suggest little else. Nothing that could whip air out of a confession or hoist temple beams; no brazen game of tug of war.

At times, done with the day's retrieving and often thinking about time—*time riding off, riding time like a moss, time as hidden mortar and pestle sense*—she stood in her garden on a cooler evening, her braid adorned with a weave of red chilli peppers. Two long sections of jute string folded and knotted together at the top to form four strands. A pepper placed horizontally over the two middle strings and under the outer strands. The inner strings pulled up and the next chilli fitted under, then the strings pulled down to the outside. The middle strings again pulled up, another pepper added under, the strings dropped to the outside. The tight pattern repeating in a delicate dance of the fingers. Marigolds towards the end and a simple utterance: *flesh is bird, flesh is curd, word is hair and flesh.*

# 3

ARTH HELPED HER FRIEND, A local artist, put up photographs in a new gallery. The space was part of a laterite fort on a hilltop on the the outskirts of town. Built and destroyed, rebuilt, ruined and abandoned by numerous rulers since the sixteenth century, it offered a grand view of the Arabian Sea and had recently received a facelift. The new look, questioned by a few but widely accepted, greatly offended the artist, who went on and on about the differences between reconstruction, restoration and preservation—how one couldn't go around sticking new noses, changing tiles or setting the stained-glass calla lilies not with traditional lead but Tiffany-style, with copper foil; how there were rules for these things. That a lower arch had been added at the fort's entrance, along with gaudy motifs and poorly painted elements that made no historical sense, frustrated him and made him wish for dereliction instead.

The photos in the gallery could have brought some comfort, for they recounted the functions served by different sections of the fort over time, but he was too caught up. Farther away from the images of the cistern and prison and closer to the hospital wing, Arth stood gazing at a door with a coin slot. Her lips tinted with the wake of a dawn ship but her head unwashed.

You'll never guess what a friend of mine adopted on her birthday, she said, cutting in.

What? he said.

The frame wasn't right, so he moved closer to correct it.

Do you smell something? he said.

Of course she could smell it.

And this tends to the chronology? he said.

She turned to him and smiled. A tsunami siren.

# 4

LUNI THREADED HER NEEDLE WITH a long strand of hair and stitched a landscape. She had set the rice to soak and now she worked on a handkerchief fixed in an embroidery hoop with a bowl resting next to her feet on the floor. In the bowl were small rings of black threads that had been untangled, rinsed in milk and water, then dried. She sat by the window of her home and stitched. Outside the window, the sea spread out at a short distance—blue grey because her hands were rubbed clean; the rice was soaking and there were hidden snaps between the buttons running down her breasts that kept the gaps safely closed. She had to keep it that way while working.

The television played loudly in the background for company. She followed a faint outline on the soft cotton—a sketch familiar to any child: a range of perfectly triangular mountains, a small sun, clouds, a house beside a stream, rocks and tall trees. The barred windows formed eyes and a toothy smile. Teeth were important. Teeth and hair, hair and teeth: two things Luni believed most sacred to a woman. She had taught her daughter how to take out knots in the dark; watched her bite to fill both thirst and hunger—a gnaw on the bone, a slow paring down or a dense, smooth chunk of deciduous plunder. She'd raised her on the story of the thieves who tore locks off bad girls and glued them together to make dolls for peace. Those pretty little pocket mascots that got shipped to every ravaged place on earth, packed in boxes with a dress-change, hung from keychains.

Pausing her stitching, Luni touched the place for snow. It was the simpler peace she wanted—not handed over or solving, but encrusted with the exhaled breath. Blood rush to the cheeks and a marvellous whitening—she'd only encountered such a scene in movies and photographs, but one day she and her daughter would go there. And there were ways to keep this desire close: shaking her hair over her knees while wearing black, threading wool through a comb, inhaling camphor, sucking on shaved ice and adding snowcaps to the mountains in the embroidery along with a snowman. Charcoal eyes, a carrot-shaped nose, sticks for arms, a muffler and a dotted smile.

A film she had seen several times before began to play on the screen, and Luni's ears grew alert to the swift shift in terrain. A camel would be shot in the slums of Mumbai. The house would drown in vinegar. She sat up straight and, without turning around, at the right time, lightly cocked her head and mouthed along to a dialogue: *saala ret ka jaanwar yahan samandar mein kaiko marne aaya?* Why did the desert animal come to the sea to die?

She bent down and selected another string from the bowl. Moistened its tip with her tongue and kept it between her lips for a while, gathering a trace, tasting across the inevitable spectrum—love, loss, loneliness—with an estrangement of an appraiser, but sometimes there was something else, something reserved from her or cleverly sheathed, something adamant—with a collar?—that moved in a fifth kind of way, a shuffling up slowly, in little waves—and when that happened, Luni rushed to spit it out.

# 5

HIMMO WAS DISTRACTED BY A pale toddler who had his legs tucked gently under the waves. She wanted to play with him, pick him up, ask him the same question she asked for every body of water: *how deep is it?* But when her friend called out to her, she promptly dismissed her thoughts and resumed focus. The rule of the game was simple: whoever found the most flip-flops on the beach within an hour got to keep them all. A pair earned a bonus point and a fizzy boot or a loafer did not count—only something a little more than a sole. The winner could choose what he wanted to do with the haul. It was Himmo's favourite activity once school was over and while her mother was still at work. She would fly off with her friends, darting along the shore for the first hint of red peeking through the ghost nets, the buried blue between the boats, the violet dressed in bits of beer bottle. She had seen it all drawn on them—cars, palm trees, mermaids, even a face that formed across a pair. Eyes, a subtle smile dragged across two touching soles and a narrow almond-shaped hole in the middle. The positioning of the flip-flops was crucial to Himmo's myth-making: facing towards the sea or turned away, the possibility of a permanent exchange.

Some of the older boys and girls would run far towards the big rocks that separated the fishing boats from the part of the beach where a swanky hotel was located, but Himmo always stayed behind, following the two things her mother had told her: stay close to home and never go into the sea unattended, for that is where creatures like them dissolved. Not drowned, she'd insisted. Dissolved. Other bodies drowned. The locusts drowned at sea. *Ghul*, she'd said. *Ghul.* We mingle and are gone, and there lies the catastrophe. Her voice had pushed the distinction beyond itself and given Himmo speed. She'd run a little further than the last parked boat, to the point from where she could still hear the concrete mixer's faint purring for the tall building coming up, then run back. She was quick to retract from the surf.

In any case, the extra stretch of sand her friends covered didn't seem to bother her because life was more alive where the hulls flaunted names. There was *Blue Diamond*, *Sea Rose*, *Kali*, *God is My Avenger* and one painted simply *D*. What the D stood for, she never wondered. She knew that if she wanted, she could start a new collection of toothbrushes or bottle caps or hair ties, stilts or masks and oars, but those were of no interest to her. Nor were the straws that could bow backwards, or the wide, straight ones. All that was waste, and she was not a waste picker. All that was for the filthy rabbit holding out his top hat, and he wasn't alone. There was the kangaroo with her pouch, the hippo with his open mouth, the penguin with his beak. The zoo trilling USE MEEEEE. They begged all day; they sought their manna and when someone obliged, by virtue of his very deed, deformed him.

For Himmo, the pleasure was only in the sport. She collected the flip-flops in a plastic bag hoisted on her shoulder, and her tally had never been zero. Her best had been six. But she had once cheated upon finding a lovely peach pair that were a bit small for her. The straps embellished with cowrie shells. She had crouched behind the shining D, lifted her dress and slipped them into her underwear.

Upon reaching home, she had put them on and twirled around, dropping to the floor to feel the slits. Shells at first shy as a bottom, then the crimped edges opening slowly. She had got up and twirled some more, her ample heels not yet unhanding.

Himmo had never won the treasure hunt.

# 6

ON THE TABLE IN FRONT of Gul was a stamp-sized picture of a male body with the stately head of a barasingha. Long, twelve-tined antlers forming a cup. God of scales. God in a flared skirt.

Gul was at the science centre, waiting for the room to fill up. It was part of a building that was foremost a cyclone shelter. The dull cream exterior blended into its surroundings, and a ramp draped the structure like a sari, connecting the first floor from the front and the second floor from the back. The science centre was on the second floor and had a main hall, two big rooms and a smaller one. The hall was a haphazardly assembled, mediocre hub of exhibits and vibrant partitions, while the rooms played host to talks, workshops and demonstrations. There were the standard skeletons, an abacus, a chart of the periodic table, a large funnel, a tightrope section and a few terrible mirrors. A left hand raised for a left, another returning ten heads for one, yet another returning none. The stark, shimmering river confounded with its abstinence, renouncing the net, and was known to send darlings scurrying to the bathroom, holding their faces in place, desperate in search of yielding water lest strange effects lingered and they found themselves to merely be a sensation, or worse, seasick in their dreams. Lest they see the ship carrying rocks at night. Then quickly to the wall with the sieve, the top half made of a finer grain than the bottom so that the lips were somewhat more visible than the eyes. There in the dim corner, the lesson on light clearly lost on them, they saw someone else's lineaments—strange, commiserating, polka-dotted—and felt instant relief, safe for further exploration.

Gul, aside from leading the earth sciences department at the main university in town, ran the centre's Geology Mondays, a session she had designed to introduce the language of the earth to visiting schoolchildren. Sometimes, she'd prepare a sweet course for the class: layer cakes, chocolate clusters, baked fossils, brownie pieces that fit together like ancient continents. Confections crunched, squished and split with sticky fingers while the projector screen came alive with mountains over the sea and the sea before the mountains. Almost never did Gul move away from the screen in time, causing the glaciers and gorges, plateaus and sinks to pour over her. She bumbled, ripped and flared, spilled a cataract, became the cradle where the wheel was born or an odd zebra of sediment. Her voice meandering more and more as she spoke till it cut off in a flood and left an oxbow. The kids would scramble to pick it up to wear around their necks so that they could look just like her. Now they could tell her that a mountain and a cloud give you rain, and mountain and mountain also give you rain. She'd stress the calculation—the measure of the wander as related to the channel's width—but a bitter morning could make it all wrong, and yet Gul carried on, and most of all, she loved talking about earthquakes. For her own story began with one—the shake that claimed her mother.

A powerful convulsion on an otherwise equable morning, when her father was away at school conducting the Republic Day parade and during which her mother had begun to push her out under a tree as buildings fell, roads got buried and cows withheld their milk. The animals had stopped days before, around the same time the hens gave up laying eggs, but not much was made of it, except that they were tired. Not harbouring any grand secret, and no witch was blamed—not even when a hen died after a day of dragging her behind—because the dogs were quiet. The farmer simply took her limp body to the back of the house, washed her down and searched her vent with his fingers for any trapped eggs. In an animal pause so deep and private, Gul was born as a sloughing of great satisfaction. By the time help arrived, her mother had woven a carpet of scarlet blossoms and died.

Gul, Gulmohar. The laden tree had witnessed the mystery at birth—the moment when the force hovered, then seeped from under into the oblivious body, transforming it into a listening fault. Tremors coursed through Gul like a memory train. *Ting ting ting. Yaatrigan kripaya dhyaan dein. For the kind attention of passengers*. Empty cans clanging out the windows. The linen man using an extra sheet to make the bed. *Ting ting ting*. Telluric fabulosity. Cities flung ten feet to the south or west; islands thrown up, then swept back under. Gul could dance those names: *Allahbund Karakoram Zalzala Koh*. And she had once—crawling, gliding, stomping her feet in her room, moving round and round like a dervish with chilli strung in her braid—for six whole minutes.

Any difficult aftermath she parked under the purview of the barasingha. Fire, flood, broken bone china; rifles driving hands to dig, which when they did, found earrings in a dead man's mouth—all that was his. He who'd raise a fist and catch every doomed breath. For her part, Gul shook most noticeably at night, discouraging anyone who wanted to share her bed. Even the smallest temblor thrilled her, and it almost always first struck her limbs. Beginning somewhere in the thighs, or calves if she was resting on her side, the waves radiating outwards. A soft rumble, a rolling, a strengthening hum, or a jerk that would wake her up with a start. Preview. Ambush. Remix. Liquor lapping freely in the drains.

# 7

ARTH HEARD HIM ALL THE TIME:

> *Come hold for a little while. Come look at the pumps, tell me what you read sixth line from the top ... Even so, even then. Look over here. Look again. The bow doors are open ...*

But the juggler stayed empty-handed until after one of Gul's crazy dishes. All those drumsticks cooked in cardamom cream, whole cashews cramped in curry. She could reason out her mother's treats for the science centre, but the occasionless richness at home shot up crystals he caught and tossed so dangerously—those fast arrangements of voices and places that slipped and shattered and lodged into the vital crevices of Gul's mind. Like the time she'd had crab roe and later found herself among the 'bagless' women of drought country. These were cane cutters. They came from their home towns and camped near the fields and, together with their husbands, each pair formed a sickle. Some of them had dropped babies out on factory floors or during long hours of hacking, binding, loading; some were in their twenties. All of them with loans to pay for the surgery. But nobody had forced them, they said. Nobody had asked them to get rid of it. Sick of the pain, infection, the contractor's fine every time they stopped too long to rest while on their period and scared of missing a single day's work, they had followed the advice of wise men or sought the cure themselves. The result was debt and a whole new set of agonies—hurting bones, sobful sleepless nights, blame from their burdened husbands—but the sugarcane women woke up, more serviceable, and went back straight to their toil, and whatever little thirst for life they had left in their eyes they planted instead and watched it grow and ask for more and more and more.

Standing outside this thirst, Arth saw the doctors arrive, streaking through the rows on a full moon night. They climbed a bare tree that stood at the edge of a field and sat on it, blowing into the wombs as though they were sugar balloons, pinching out a leg or two or four, a snout, ears, some fins, even a stem of leaves. Juggler speech:

*Now see that's cracked a little. Time to find a substitute!*

It was this part, this act of searching for what had finally but so scarcely given up, the long neck or shell, then copying the break's pattern in ink, that had registered the tiniest shard's brutal angle, something jammed inside like an invisible guitar pick, and sent Arth rushing to the kitchen to check if the stove was off. She had looked down to also check the cylinder. She had done it multiple times, going to her room and coming back, switching the lights on and off, until she finally took a picture of the knobs to remember.

Fortunately, shortly after, Arth figured out a way to recover more sustainably, or at the very least, give nothing away during meals. One day, a boy stumbled out from between a man and woman in black and proceeded to trail her. Like a signature practised on the back pages of a notebook in anticipation of the world, he stuck around. Arth didn't contest his presence at first because of the safe distance, but then the hours grew darker and there was a sense of closing in. Daunted by his fullness, she tried wishing him away, fired at him with questions, and when nothing worked, wrote him a message:

*Your tipping and flicking, your cups by the hem*
*There no more by the soldier clad in flee*
*I'd like a real gift instead.*

The boy had taken her words and bounced back into the gap; Arth had felt an ebbing. From then on, she wrote to whichever chalky one showed up. She did not feel the urge to pull the tablecloth or retch into the food. Did not want to fling the fruit bowl. She sat next to her mother, who was always at the head of the table, setting the pace, which, if it could speak, would say: *Watch me satisfy a craving. Watch us fall in love with our rescue.* Once or twice, when the light fuzz on Arth's leg grazed against her mother, she retracted instantly, but did not stop eating. She'd pop a pill if it became too much, later sitting on the pot for hours. She'd consume it all till she felt a pimpling inside. The same old voice. *Here's a plate for your bones, here's a plate—GO STICK YOUR CHOPSTICKS SOMEPLACE ELSE!*

# 8

THERE WAS A LULLABY IN the air at eleven in the morning, but no one among the crowd seemed to hear it. Women in bright tops clustered at the best spots to take pictures; children gambolled around licking lollies. A few men lingered on the fringes for a sign of blood, sweat or tears. One touch and they left their dust on fingertips, which the gullible rubbed on their eyelids and lips. Had the shimmering men been more curious and not avoided the dogs darting between the legs of people close to the water, they would have seen what all the fuss was about: a giant, dead fish.

An old woman walked up and placed a child on the body. The girl wanted to ride the fish home. But a volunteer with the forest department swiftly plucked her off.

Are you crazy? she snarled at the woman. You want to go to jail?

A young fisherman pushed his way to the front to get a closer look. He had never seen anything like it before. Starved dolphins, yes; turtles with cracked shells after a storm, yes; a tern with a broken beak—but never the creature. Broad, flat head; skin striped and dotted with stars. Benign ocean smile.

Why is this whale here? someone shouted.

The volunteer shook her head. It's not a whale, it's a whale shark, she shouted back.

It looks like a whale.

But it's a shark. A fish. *Rhincodon typus.* Not a whale, not a mamm—

The man had already turned the camera on himself.

The policemen and forest authorities initially tried pushing the group back closer to the boats, but soon gave up. An officer picking his nose joked about a case on the east coast where municipal authorities had pitched a tent and charged people to view the carcass of a whale shark accidentally caught in a net.

I heard it was pregnant when they pulled it up, he said. They left it hanging on the side of the boat. At least we don't do *that*.

The vet arrived to record the body's preliminary measurements. Its tail and fins were missing. The volunteer carried on with facts about the species: the biggest fish in the sea, gentle filter feeders, thick-skinned, big mouth, small throat, slow but can swim long distances—a tagged one set a record by travelling more than 20,000 kilometres in about two and a half years across the Pacific ...

She stopped to imagine the feat, but what came to mind was her own father walking along the beach, morning and evening, counting on his rosary of a hundred beads. It had roughly taken him the same amount of time to realize that those beads were actually Job's tears.

The vet declared his observations: a juvenile male. Length four and a half metres, girth three metres.

The volunteer parted the crowd and left in search of a soft serve. Anything but sham strawberry.

By the time she returned to the spot, it was twilight and the fish was gone. It had been hauled up and buried at an undisclosed location after a postmortem. In its place, away from the waves, was a sand sculpture of the beast. Its tail and fins intact. Around it lay flowers, food wrappers, plastic cups and burning candles. The volunteer stood by the eye hole on one corner of its head for a while, then walked into the water. She thought about the crowd earlier. There had been a forehead. A dotless, floating forehead. She felt the sand cave in and, through the balls of her feet, she drew—through the dot—a culmination, a viscid heartbeat.

# 9

THE WHOOSH SETS THE INWARD curl—Luni was confident of it without looking. The sights and sounds of the beauty parlour nourished her. The gaggle to touch the first moustache; the halo spritzed in threes, as if a rushed fourth could curb the drain. On the cashier's desk was a pamphlet of all the services provided:

Waxing
Chocolate Waxing
Threading
Facial
Bleach
Hair Spa
Hair Cut
Hair Colour
Head Massage

Body Polishing
Manicure
Pedicure
Makeup
Mehendi

This list was a shorter one, changed after the board outside, which was supposed to say UNISEX, lost its 'I' and the parlour began receiving only female customers. It had happened well before Luni joined, and in this world for women, she was what they called an all-rounder. She was authorized to do everything on the list except for snipping hair. That was a task for the Ammonias, the three men on call. Almost indistinguishable in their black shirts and aprons, they'd been dubbed so because of the bizarre need of one of the early recruits to fiercely sniff paint pots in order to clear a cold. While the beauticians mostly followed instructions, the realm of the Ammonias was priestly, filled with steady notes of persuasion and cautious pleas.

Not too short.

Can be shorter.

I'll go around and thin some more.

Look down please.

A flatter edge?

No, this wouldn't work.

If blonde looked good, God would give us blonde.

I have a wedding coming up.

You'll have to bleach.

Then, on one of those days strummed with the compassion of husks, a girl getting her feet bathed had looked at a card and whispered, *ash ash ash.* Cuticles swelling for their first brush with colour, wisps of reaped hair blowing off laps and a sweeper sweeping after herself, pausing only to wipe the shelves. The Ammonias towering above all, presiding over the flow, conducting hands to bunch, scrunch, scrape and squeeze, wash twice before or after and sell all the while. Dab with one finger. Don't pull too much. Sell spas, strips and fragrant oils, bottles of shampoo and conditioner. Lather, lather faded brown, wine iridescent, make it creamy, ease the necks up. Mother and daughter leaning with their heads tipped back into the sinks, mother lulled to sleep but the daughter still small and therefore elevated on a hard cushion, her eyes wide open, staring at the light above, which bounces off her cheeks. What's to be done if a child's reckoning comes before yours. Staring at the light but not into blinding light, no movement from light to dusk. The youngest Ammonia enters wearing section clips on his sleeves and a scent called 'Wildfire' that makes the birds lift their cries, find their range.

Time's up. Time for a cut again. Dress the wound with aftershave.

Then, at last, recognition of the blade's will.

Got cut too short.

Oh well.

But before the conclusion, it was Luni who would often show the cut, a job which, on most days, she took very seriously. There were no draft mirrors, so to trap a charge between two of them was a brave and powerful act. The woman could easily lose, even if just for a few seconds, her sense of witness. The loss could be dangerous, could kick her into chaos, and only if the angles were delicate and Luni wasn't moody with it, could the terror subside almost amicably.

She led a customer further into the parlour for a head wash.

Does this feel alright, madam? she asked, pouring lukewarm water.

Hm.

The beige wall facing them had a poster of a starlet, a former Miss World. Luni did not care for the photo;

the gloss was in bad taste. The workers at the parlour could make a world with their tints and methods but not come close to her, never her. Luni preferred the picture closer to the entrance, above the cashier's desk, of a stone carving of a woman—features chipped away—wearing large earrings and an intricate beehive. The hair decorated with beads and medallions, like a temple rising. Its height astounded her and she would often ask her clients to spare a look while making payments. Now she set to work on the scalp in front of her, her hands doing what they could never be paid for: spotting the crumble of a woman, squeezing out the tightness and years from the neck of one who could not conceive. Who had looked up photographs of C-section scars and scraped a bloody one out for herself. Luni had held her and pressed her till the sobs ceased.

She let the foam gather under her client's earlobes while her hands rested on the porcelain. The clink of her bangle on the sink took her to the chains at the ghat. Nowadays, one could hire a dipper for ten rupees and collect penance. A double-dip for just fifteen. She wondered about the shape of her mercy. Then suddenly, the women in the parlour began rotating their chairs towards the television, and Luni leaned sideways to look with them.

A shaky video was up on the screen, of a few glistening men wielding knives in the dark, torches shining through the pockets of their wet shorts, cutting off the fins of the whale shark. One kneeling in the waves for better control. No voices. Horrendous music in the background. From a small box on the side of the screen, a reporter announced rather forcefully that the creature had been breathing during the assault.

What a crazy lip, someone said. So distracting.

Though Luni couldn't fully see a row of customers from behind the sink, their voices floated over to her.

Nowadays, they slap on anything.

Look, the blouse is also so tight.

Remember the noodle straps?

What an era that was.

But that was a sports channel.

Isn't there some sort of code for this?

The video played repeatedly, starting and stopping at different frames marked with harsh circles.

These men, they don't look like they're from here.

How can you tell?

Oh, come on, you can tell. An impatient finger wagged at the screen. They have their backs to the sea.

Luni cleared her throat and washed quickly. She wrapped a towel around her customer's head and led her to a seat. Then she adjusted the height of the chair.

Five minutes and I will apply the cream, madam, she said. We have a few magazines in the drawer.

But the woman was already engrossed in the news. She was watching it through the mirror.

Luni returned to pick up the hair lining the basin. She washed the strands in water, gathered them in a small bunch, then very quietly slipped the bunch into the pocket of her apron. Quality control was important for the threads she used in her embroidery. Only fallen hair found loose on towels, pillows and drains, tubs, soaps, sinks, combs and rubber bands. Not cut, shaved or plucked hair. Only strands that had done their bidding like days gone. Only black, undyed strands. Because blackness was understood by white cotton. Blackness as donned by the veiled mourners who shed tears for the dead of others with sounding boards in their chests, only to be treated as lesser folks bearing sons of princes. If they bore daughters, they expanded their tribe. Luni knew she could carve a dream out of such a night.

She mixed a few drops of serum into a bowl of repairing hair mask and began to paint it on her client's head.

What do you make of the news? the woman asked, adjusting the black cape around herself.

She hooked a finger inside the neck hole to keep it loose. On her phone screen was an article about the whale shark in a national daily written by a certain Ms Jaffrey whose bio read: Has covered flora, fauna and the rape of the florist.

Luni shrugged her shoulders. I don't know, madam. I didn't see the whale.

It was not a whale. It was a shark.

Oh.

It's an endangered species.

Luni kept quiet.

It is a crime to kill it under the Wildlife Protection Act.

Did they find it on the beach?

I don't know.

Did it lose its way?

Don't know.

Could it have gulped a lot of sand? Did they drag it to the beach?

The woman glared at her. Doesn't matter. They killed it.

Her deep-set stare reminded Luni of the lawyer who had saved her home from getting razed a few months ago. She had secured a physical copy of the stay order in the nick of time and pushed back the authorities who declared the neighbourhood too close to the sea, within the limits of the hazard zone, when the real reason for their actions was the new road and building coming up. Most of the evicted were domestic workers, small fishermen whose families had lived in the town for generations, and labourers who worked on the boats. For those confirmed as traditional fishermen by the state, the officers assured there would be rehabilitation at a later stage.

But what about those legals over there? the lawyer had said, pointing to the hotel on the other side. Does the water not rise for them?

A few reporters had come along for a tour. They had jotted frantic notes, their cameras greedy for the most vivid piece of ruin. Leading them to the middle of the neighbourhood, she had asked the newsmen to be careful around a narrow strip on the ground—an arrangement of the residents' voter cards displaying their addresses. A long shadow blade.

But no amount of publicity could stop the bulldozer now, whose wrath was only intensifying. Houses were being decapitated in the middle of the night, notices slipped under doors just as the courts shut down for holidays. The khakis came in riot gear alongside trucks and excavators. The elders squatted and watched the rubble drop. The drivers of the heavy machinery wary of their dumb stares: *You can go home now.*

On her way back from work, Luni thought about how reckless it would get during the rains. She stopped outside a house not too far away from where she lived. It was her lover's abode, where she had spent several hours mounting him and unleashing her mane from a plastic claw. False bends quickening: bothered into being. Filling them up, giving them names. In the beginning, her period had brought them quite a fever and a bright, brittle star. Soon after, she had made him a white lace glove—with a scallop trim and a tiny white bow at the wrist—which he wore on his left hand to stroke her all over. Come rein or shine. Come smug rain. Pinching, pivoting till they took the form of a russet filly, and then the collapse, after which they would lie, his head on her stomach, drifting. When it was time to leave, Luni would put her hair up, dust her chest and collarbone with talcum powder and walk home.

Now only concrete fragments survived in that space, one of the many irregular gaps in the dense row of houses. Damp clothes hung on a line between the remnants. Each razed home, every chamber of love and worship that was destroyed, marked with prayer flags.

# 10

HIMMO'S CLOSEST FRIEND, A few years older than her, won a round of the flip-flop game and decided to share his victory. He took her along to visit the junk dealer, but the usual skinny man was not at his shop. Instead, there was a round, elderly fellow with a tangerine beard sitting beside a three-legged lampstand among piles of newspapers, magazines, refrigerators and other household appliances. He wore a die on his upper right arm over his tight-fitting kurta and looked in desperate need of a conversation. Seeing the children approaching, his neck popped up, and he quickly shifted the Bisleri bottles filled with petrol to one side of the counter.

Look who's here! I have been waiting a long time. Now what have you brought me?

We want to sell these, the boy said, handing him a bag of flip-flops.

The man opened it and sifted through the contents, then lifted it to approximate the weight. He put it on a scale, took out his money box and counted two notes of ten and seven one-rupee coins.

Just short of thirty, he said.

That's alright, said the boy, holding out his hand.

But wait, wait, what's the hurry? I have a deal for you.

The old man paused, then leaned over the counter and pointed at the shells on Himmo's feet.

Give me that pair, and you can have thirty rupees and something very special.

Himmo hid behind the boy. Loud, grown men disturbed her and she didn't exactly know why, but her mother said it was a 'God Gift' the day she had dashed under the bed during a visit from someone from the neighbourhood. Luni had not tried to coax her out, explaining to the man instead, who soon became a frequent presence at home. From her space, Himmo grew accustomed to his long legs and clean, solid feet enclosed in the same worn-out pair of brown sandals, which encouraged her to improve the rest of him, including his sound, and thereby drove her to pity. A feeling that grew stronger each time he visited until she could take it no more and had to step out and face him as he was. Now this stranger's voice was stroking the same need for cover.

But they don't even fit, the old man said, and the legs of the lamp grew longer. That the flip-flops were a bit small for her didn't matter; what did was how they gently nudged the eyes to kiss the ground she stood on. Many people had even commented on her toenails, offering to paint them. In the bland romance of rags and a freedom song, she had found something beautiful, and she would not give them up for anything an adult deemed special.

What do you have? she asked, fixing her gaze on the Bisleri bottles. Not knowing the difference, she thought the liquid in them was kerosene or *Hassassunum*, as one of the neighbourhood aunts had taught her. Because it laughs when it burns.

The old man nodded. Hold on.

He wobbled into the shop and retrieved a pouch from one of the shelves. Then he came back with one hand inside the drawstring purse, rummaging in it. At first, pulling his hand out and wincing, as though pricked by what was inside, then putting it back again and pulling out a headband.

The children gasped. It was stunning. A thin, black velvet frame studded with little white globes.

These are pearls, he said. You know what pearls are?

The children shook their heads.

They are precious jewels found deep in the ocean. They are made by sea creatures.

Creatures as big as that fish? the boy asked.

The old man's eyes sparkled. Did you get to see it?

The boy's hand shot up like it did in school.

I didn't, but my mother told me it was an important fish, Himmo said.

The old man nodded. It must have been. But no, these animals are smaller.

What do you think happened to it? asked Himmo.

The old man sighed. Must have stayed awake too long.

Are these expensive? the boy asked.

Yes, he said. Now put it on. Let us see.

Himmo tightened her ponytail and placed the band on her head. She looked into the mirror held up by the junk dealer and fell in love with what she saw. There were a few beads missing from the top, but that didn't bother her.

At night, it will look like you're wearing all the moons.

But something wasn't adding up for the boy. If the pearls are so precious, why are you giving them to us?

Do you want it or not? said the old man sternly.

The boy glanced at Himmo. Look like naphthalene balls to me.

She bent down and reached for her footwear. A quick dust, a sniff and she let them go. Her friend took the money, and the two turned to leave when the old man called out again.

I have something else as well! Bring me another nice pair and you can have it!

Himmo didn't look back. All the moons, she whispered under her breath as she walked barefoot. Not one. All. In the dark, she would float in their inverted bowl of light. One by one, she would name them. Snow Moon. Crow's Sorrow.

# 11

*TO THE PIANIST PLAYING IN church at lunchtime—*

*You came on in your silk shirt, but where's the blush? The* harsingar*? The teeth marks on the wood? Must be the fog of a few too many standing ovations.*

*It's a praise for the milkman; it's an embankment breach.*

*In any case, just finger it.*

# 12

GUL SAT UP IN BED with the stench of rotting blubber in her throat. She breathed into her cupped palm and the smell bounced back into itself, pulling her along and there she was again: watching a whale explode. A beached mammal blown apart using explosives, flesh hailing down, tainting everything. Spectators awed as though it were a fireworks show. Hands and faces sprayed with blood, bone, detritus; children catching the drizzle in their dry mouths gaped open. A man dodging a lump, then kicking it like a football.

There's more. People at the same location some years later bring flowers and set up tables on the dunes. Visitors order plates of cold beet salad, buttery potatoes and lamb devoted to a mint sauce. A whole roasted head of cauliflower dressed in raisins and pomegranate seeds. Custard with cookie crumbs for dirt. A woman laughs sweetly, watching her child crawl after an eggplant. She touches the ribbon on her shoulder—a snippet from a finish line—and sings. *Baby but the whales don't fall like snow.* Beside her, a painter with a covered throat tries unsuccessfully to render the sea and in front of them all, the ghost mammal lying on the sand, panting, waiting ...

Somewhere in the deep, cold waters, a cow is being lowered into a canyon. Gul had looked up at this point, from which body she could not remember. No birds come to steal the bread.

# 13

THE UNDERWIRE IS PERHAPS A girl's first personal lesson in border-making. Long after the mark is gone, the soul remains a victim of the sad red line. What endures is the moment when the line becomes both metal and flesh, the flesh participating in the steady violence she is taught to hold close in order to lift, support, shape, separate, govern and make attractive, and this opens her up to the wider meanness of the Radcliffe Line, the 38th parallel, the LAC, the Durand Line. To forsake it is to embrace a certain lawlessness, which Arth had done, but not fully. The wireless replacement she had on oppressed in the heat and ridiculed her insecurities, making her want to take everything off at once.

It was one of those afternoons when flyaways from bobby pins aggravated and just fifteen minutes outside was too much. Arth and the artist had suffered the weather only to outdo the distracted couple sitting next to them on the fort's parapet before rushing off to the photo gallery. Arth's hair was up in a small knot and she stood in front of a pedestal fan, shaking her T-shirt, waiting for her friend to speak.

The artist, seated on a chair, was watching a man follow the turning head of the other fan in the room. Right to left, left to right. Arth did not know him to be so quiet. They had met on the beach at an event organized by a citizen's group to map the high tide line and hit it off instantly. Pairing up, talking the whole time as they gathered data and took photos of scum lines, objects and seaweed fragments at different locations that marked the waves' furthest ingress. The observations, later collated and analysed, had confirmed that if the line was mapped accurately on the hotel's side of the beach, it would fall within the property's compound.

How perfect! The artist had thrown his hands in the air. Their line dives right into the sea!

That it bent was not as shocking as the degree to which it bent in the reports submitted to the court by the coastal authorities. The hotel had been called out in a public interest litigation for violation of the hazard zone and encroachment on the beach and, in the reports, an entirely new criteria had been invented for drawing the line. As Arth had listened to her friend talk about slippery scientists and government officials, her mind wandered off to editors. Their hand so aggressive sometimes and, at its worst, downright erosive. *Make it clear or make it glow. Style the cast or crop the leg.* And since a line troubled could only lead to the knee, she and the artist had sat for hours on the rocks segregating the beach, looking out at the waves and discussing not just any knees but the knees of shipwrecks.

All kinds—hanging knee, lodging knee, dagger, breasthook, grown, braced, standing knee, painted knee, laminated knee—fated for the deep ocean floor or given not even that, just the brutal swipe of wind and water. And then not just any wreck, but the artist's beloved *Jhelum*, whose features he'd nailed with a softness: flat-bottomed and not known for speed, keel made of rock elm, keelson of African oak, frames of English oak, beams of English and African oak, lower planking of rock elm, above-water planking of hackmatack and African hardwoods, decking of yellow pines and hackmatack. Copper fastened and spiked with iron, she was ditched by her crew in a harbour somewhere after she'd struggled around the Horn with a load of bird poo.

This one, he'd said, brimming. This one got custom knees. Been sitting and posing for over a century. Now the birds poop on whatever's left.

Arth had smiled. Give a name different deaths and see what it keeps. The form, folding unfolding, only attempts to meet it. It could be helpful then, she thought, to tell oneself that these are my knees and this is my kneeling through it all, not before or after anything, just my kneeling. Let them date it all they want.

But what's innate and pre-existing is never easy to look at, and perhaps that is why the state had commissioned a light-and-sound show at the fort, which the artist was adamant he'd taken up only for the money, because the brief resembled a tasteless disco party with neon pink and green beams drenching the site and bouncing in the night sky. A rare consideration in place of yet another bust or double pedestal or the relabelling of yet another park to Coconut Park (justified because the gods here, instead of globes, held coconuts). So what if work on the warning towers and a new shelter was two years behind and bus stops were without shade nets; cultural renewal had its own place. The state's suave tourism minister had announced the project in an interview and added that 'the town, and the nation as a whole, cannot rise just by the brute force of her steel and brick and mortar. There has to be soul to her rising as well.' And an exceptional soul at that, for 'unlike the aesthetics of some writers of the West, she has no register for ugliness, only *soundarya*—beauty, wisdom and colour'. Arth sighed. A soul without horror can sing such a song of spite. During one of their conversations, she and the artist had wondered what they would do if the money came unconditionally. Arth had suggested going back to the concept of the arch and doing something with it, maybe try conjoining two, one-half golden and one-half blue, but the artist had his own idea: three spoons of salt on a conveyor belt.

Now, less sweaty than before, she wanted to ask what kind of spoons but could not do so. He was still watching the man follow the fan from left to right. When he finally spoke, the artist sounded waterlogged.

It's my intern, he said.

You have an intern?

Just a kid helping me with research. Kind of brilliant, actually. Has this whole thing about two stakes ...

He pulled out a piece of newspaper from his shirt pocket and unfolded it. Arth stared at the photo of a boy in a missing person's appeal. Face: Round Complexion: Shallow Build: Medium. His eyes precariously balancing stones somewhere; if only she could draw long, thick lashes on those eyes.

The artist was rubbing his forehead. He hesitated for a moment, then pulled out another piece of paper.

His mother gave this to me, he said. Found it on his desk.

First, the writing came rolling in gently, then the words hit:

~~THE TWO-STAKE THEORY OF UNSUBSCRIBE~~
CALL ME HOW TELL TONIGHT
CALL ME PHILOMEL TONIGHT

We fed the whale
We fed the whale a greenhouse
We fed the whale a greenhouse
We fed the whale a greenhouse
We fed the whale a greenhouse
We fed the whale a greenhouse
We fed the whale a greenhouse
We fed the whale a greenhouse
We fed the whale a greenhouse
We fed the whale a greenhouse
We fed the whale a greenhouse

We fed the whale a greenhouse
We fed the whale a greenhouse
We fed the whale a greenhouse
The sea stars killed themselves

# 14

LUNI EXAMINED THE HEADBAND AND breathed a sigh of relief. The pearls were balls of plastic. She knew better than to let her daughter wear real ones after she had found out how they were made at a farm during a visit with a friend from work.

The woman's brother employed there had explained the entire process. How they'd pick a live oyster and pry it open just enough to insert a small bead or an image along with a sliver of foreign tissue inside. The invaded creature, unable to eject the object, then secreted thousands of layers of shiny coating around it to protect itself, resulting in a jewel over time.

Luni's cheeks tingled at the thought of the shells being discarded or reused. It triggered the memory of a sky-blue dress embroidered with silver peacock pairs. She had wanted to look different in a colour other than red. Her mother had insisted that she at least peel apples under her veil during the ceremony, and she had agreed but then forgotten her knife in the chaos of the wedding. Looking back, there had been so many mistakes. A distant aunt had pinned her in excess. She also hadn't visited the local shrine prior to the day as per ritual and offered a clock.

With a simple mind, Luni had loved the dress until the heat licked all the ulcers at once and brought with it repeated rage for her beauty; bleating goats and cattle dying of stroke; thighs thrust wide open. Parts smelling like fruit cooked on the branch, scorched flesh to the pit, too soft for the mouth of the caretaker. Sharp, black fingernail that grew not straight but curved, like a talon, inside her. Semen sliding down her lips to her chin as she held her baby to her chest, her kurta taut under her knees. She could never stomach him, not even when she'd wanted to, when things had been fine. She never wished she had stuck with a red dress.

To block the flashes out, Luni focused on how different the heat felt by the seaside, how it plugged in more like a lament. But the effort left her exhausted, which she tried to conceal from her six-year-old who was putting the beads back on her head.

Himmo, her only child, whom she believed she had held in two days longer, just so that she could run away from the clinic where she had been deposited to give birth, sitting in a chair in a line of groaning, protruding women, with no one from the family around to even offer water. Some of the women beginning to push out heads and legs right there in the seats and the one doctor who had finally arrived and slapped a delivering woman, not for making a mess but for not screaming loud enough.

What if you or your baby die? Then we are the ones who'll be caught in a case.

Luni had fled from that miserable place, holding her stomach, until she had reached her parents' home, where she had given birth under the loving gaze of her mother, who had wiped her brows and blown on her face while the midwife pulled the patient baby out.

Himmo, whose crumbs had widened the desert, made it even mightier. Luni remembered the day she had felt it happen—her nursing baby next to a ball of fur had rubbed her morning eyes and the grains fell quietly, the sheets rippled and swelled. The vast sand pushing past the edge of green meant to contain it, castrating fruit trees. It had been an awesome feeling, one that let her view the bird's clap mid-flight over the row of rocks leaning backwards, like teeth pointing to the throat, with a sense of deep reverence. And when night came and brought along the serpent with a head on either end, a tongue flicking to its own scent and the brilliant sky with a band of white so willing as a wet nurse, she knew that if she ever left, she would have to try very hard, battle every day to keep this land cordial. As it happened, the complex feeling did not survive long, and the humiliating fear that the dunes wanted more and sought every way to steal back her daughter convinced Luni she had to do all she could to save the girl's rain.

Himmo, unaware of her mother's thoughts, was elated that there was no objection to the headband. She had told Luni that she'd found it on the beach and the flip-flops had come apart while playing. She wore the band everywhere, even to school. Once, when she wore it to sleep, the bedsheet sparkled, and soon she saw pearls littered on the beach, bumping shyly in the breeze. One was the size of a tennis ball and she picked it up and saw the most electric blue eyes of tiny, formless creatures inside. She put it down, picked another one, and the same blue gaze seeped in deep and easy. Himmo was about to pick a third when the pearls began rolling into the sea, further and further away and down, till they touched the dark bottom and turned sheer. Then, inflating their hoods and growing thin ribbon legs, they rose like rain in reverse to form the moon. She twirled in this rain with the toddler she'd seen the other day sitting in the waves, and the water turned bronze and there were pearls studded on the horns of oxen emerging from silvery shoals of fish. She and the boy held hands and twirled, till one let go and Himmo awoke, the tips of her hair somehow wet, feeling a strong tug towards that forbidden body in her backyard.

How succulent the early insurrections of the mind.

Her friends did not fail to tell her how beautiful she looked with the band on. They begged her to lend it for a little while, but Himmo refused. She had only allowed her mother to touch it once.

Snubbed, a girl had hit back. Who wants it anyway! You look like you have teeth growing out of your head.

But the comment did nothing to faze Himmo. Squeezing out more toothpaste and brushing longer to match the lustre of the pearls, she learnt to hold her own weather in her mouth. Weather liminal and uncontrolled by anyone else: minty on top, minty on the bottom, a little sluggish at first or heavy in the corners, moderately freaky until gorgeous, or simply unhindered. Finally, an inch of daylight.

She also found an ingenious use for a pencil: hold it between the teeth and there's the smile.

Himmo paraded the pearls around and, even when she took off the band to wipe the beads, she felt it sitting behind her ears. She prodded the elders in the neighbourhood for stories and heard most about the king who plucked the freshest pearls from the sea for the white spider lilies in his garden, enticing them to bloom—to wrap their slender, white petals-like legs around the gems and push them down their throats. Himmo now longed to visit the hotel's side of the beach where women wore pearls dangling from their ears or wrapped around their necks and wrists, or as buttons down their thin blouses while they bounced on the biggest pearls ever seen. She'd heard of them laughing by the pool, laying their hands upon expensive items at the gift shop, riding up and down a golden elevator. What a thing it would be to slide a foot in the capsule and watch the grand doors shudder. On that side of the curve, she knew there were no awkward levitators. Those women could just press a pearl for rapture.

# 15

IN THE UNIVERSAL MIND, THE habit sat easefully next to the green-bangled hand under the pyre, sifting for bits. Arth spent each morning looking through the papers for details that kept the news distinct. Whether it was something central to the story or just a bit of flare didn't matter. Only the specials—Women's Day, Children's Day—she used for lining her shelves (except for a page from an Earth Day supplement with the long piece on crevice gardening. That she kept aside.) She took her time with the sheets, spreading them out on her desk, scanning and cutting fragments: monkeys puking in the library, the prosecutor choosing chicken for a lighter meal, the rioter's penchant for tabla. The gang that stole a bus stop, then a whole train engine piece by piece within a week, then a bridge. The runner who finished the race and kept on running. The homeless woman, who was arrested so she could be saved from the cold, had worn a dirty white bow; the man who took a mattress down the flood, singing. Yes, him. She kept his picture right on top in her folder. Arth closed her eyes and watched him wandering down the dark river high for his ride, whitening under him. His dark fingers parting her. If it were not for the touching of the small, clotted place, which he left untied, he could have been sipping white off the sky.

This activity of searching the papers also helped balance the effects of the big blocks of public service announcements, for instance, the frequent suicide prevention campaign for young adults, which shouted what was common between Arth and the missing boy—both in the age group 'most drawn to despair'.

Whales carved on forearms, pills taken for sleep, breaking under grades, hanging for love, throwing acid and burning from it not once or twice, but five times. Arth had read about the girl who danced all night around the bonfire of her own leg. She knew women who had saved trees but had forgotten how to scream.

But hadn't the leader clarified? *Take your own life—I meant live.* The leader of the Art of Outliving. To live out. Take your life. To out the living. To live an outing.

To beat the prognosis. To escape the war. To stay behind. To stay stranded in the sex like the finest forced dove. To leave. To live. Break out. Outlive. The word had a hazy blue light inside that swam along the surface.

Arth believed that one should leave for the night. That way, the breath did not change on the words 'do anything to survive', at least not in the time when one was conscious of breathing. Staying with her mother had taught her that much about the saved. Whether you close your eyes in every family photograph or count the trains, put on perfume when the noose breaks or shake—everybody leaves for the night of boolean buoys. So had the boy forgotten or did he not know? Or had he stopped to ponder the two ways one watches a flood—a man standing on a heap of bodies, holding on to a temple bell, and a woman waiting, with her dead six-month-old strapped to her chest. What changes in the gaze? Does the difference lie between waiting and holding on? Or in the placement of the corpse?

The questions were nagging Arth when she heard Gul call out for her.

—

Evening had begun to dwindle and she stood in a soft lime nest in front of the long rectangular mirror of her dresser. Arth entered the room and first saw the colour of Medusa's jacket. A trail marker for climbers who had to step over her legs to reach the top of Everest. Or had they already moved her? Arth leaned on the bed and tried to move on from such thoughts, but the night was fishing with magnets and she got picked by the dresser. It was cluttered with jewellery, tubes and tubs of lotion, glosses and balms. There were combs, a compact and an array of hair oils—coconut, castor, almond, amla, black cumin—stored in glass bottles, and all mixed together in one without a label. The view of the dark, stark liquid keeping vigil like an unexploded ordnance thrust at Arth an answer she did not want: not all of Gul's hair was her own.

She had built a museum of hair, buying obnoxious amounts in bundles and boxes, in different lengths and textures: synthetic hair, horsehair, Indian hair, Indonesian hair. No sale was spared. Arth saw the clutter but said nothing. Her mother looked beautiful. Waft of sandalwood. More beautiful than she herself could ever look, without Gul's height or slender figure. Clothes sat softly on her mother.

Where's the reception? Arth asked and was startled to hear her scraped voice.

You know where, Gul answered without looking up. She was folding the pleats of her sari.

Ah yes. The aquarium by the sea.

Arth had visited it at the hotel, and indeed it was a mesmeric place. When the main lights in the hall were turned off and there was only the lit glass wall, then the blue bent in its lust for water and made the bridge tick. Even the staffers halted, in their whale ties and silly octopus hats, and watched it swim past the shark over shimmering grass, or beside the specially bred clownfish, the one with a brilliant green spot—what did they call it? Picasso? Gatsby? And there were real corals, not like the box at the Tibetan restaurant she frequently visited, which had a printed wallpaper glued inside. Why wouldn't you then wheel in a very sick child and let him tap the bubbles; why wouldn't you marry it—not the guy in front—knowing at least the blue could last.

When she had told the artist about her visit, he nodded and said, Yes, but go back for the mermaid. She's a good one and they have her in the tank sometimes. She knows. Look her in the eye and play rock-paper-scissors. Then you'll know.

And so Arth had gone and played with a beautiful blonde girl in a shining purple tail, round after round, for some semblance of knowledge:

Rock paper scissors.
Rock paper scissors.
Paper covers rock.
Scissors cut paper.
Rock breaks scissors.

Rock paper scissors.
Stone water glass.
Stone water glass.
Glass keeps water.
Water sinks stone.
Stone beats the bird.
Glass beats the bird.
Rock paper scissors.
Rock paper scissors.

And then it was done. Braced by the words, she had climbed, little bird with stone clung to her chest, up above the buildings, over the waves, to the hanging woods in the sky, and from there, looking down upon the shore's length, she had seen—paper conquering rock; rock splitting the land; glass taming water; scissors cutting and seized; water waiting, waiting. She did not physically visit the aquarium after that, and ignored her mother's provocation when she said, It can't be that serious. Didn't a woman invent it? Now pressing sideways against a pillow, Arth asked Gul to bring back a wind chime.

Gul nodded. She squinted as she looked into the mirror, adjusting her sleeveless blouse, aware of the unwanted gap between skin and fabric. Her eyes were lined with bitumen night and a cream rose marked the end of her braid. Finally, she chose the drop earrings Arth had worn at a college festival years ago and, before leaving, turned and pulled her daughter up.

Dinner's in the casserole, she said. I've made fresh gunpowder.

Arth's eyes traced her mother's neck, the stem of a slightly bent tulip. She suddenly saw a much younger Gul arching back over a boulder, her hands inside kitten heels, translating the sky, with a red rock perched on her throat. Two days after the picnic, the boulder had split down the middle and the location was cordoned off.

Listen to me, Gul said. No, look at me. You will not check again and again. I ha—

Just go, Arth snapped, pushing her mother's arms away from her.

—

One night, well after twelve, Gul had watched her daughter walk to the kitchen fourteen times to check if the stove and cylinder were off. She had blitzed mango into a thick dip for dinner earlier, knowing fully well the redness that would roar after. A dark patch on the back of Arth's neck. *Sunset burn little burn.* She had watched her daughter walk back again from the stove and said nothing.

# 16

*To the form in the steam of the soup:*

*I have been making scenes out of the haze lately—*

*In the background, a child stands in a calcite-coated cave, facing a panel of big red dots arranged in the shape of an animal body.*
*In the foreground is a set of restaurant tables.*

*(Enter Bugs Bunny, dressed in a three-piece suit and a bowtie, and a chorus of four generations of a famine. They stand amidst the tables.)*

BUGS: Table for whom? Three and a half or two?

CHORUS: Two-thirds.

BUGS: It'll blow in your soup.

CHORUS: It'll brew you a red kiss.

(*The child paints her palm red and slaps it on the cave wall. Not happy with the imprint, she draws two extra fingers with charcoal. Then, slowly, she exits.*)

(*A pitcher is lit on a table, sculpted like a section of an elephant trunk. A few moments later, the real creature appears in the background, its dead body etched with 'Paddy Thief Bin Laden'*)

BUGS (*singing*): We got cooking a Bugs Bunny bunting,
Father's gone a-hunting,
just to get a rabbin skin—

CHORUS: But now the rabbit's born again!

BUGS (*singing louder, triumphantly*): To wrap the baby in!

(*Near the young elephant's feet, Copycat and Smiley, Smiley and Copycat, put down an offering of eternity roses. Neither of the two make it to the dessert course.*)

# 17

LUNI HAD LEARNT THE COAST'S flesh and barter as quickly as one learns to stand up at sea. The women of the neighbourhood had welcomed her with their cheeks sucked in and mouths pouting, a hand placed on top of the other and wiggling thumbs. Most of them were wives and daughters of fishermen and ran stalls at the fish market; others were cooks, cleaners, wives of labourers. They had taught her to suck on a thin lemon slice to bear the smell of the market, but never to cover her nose and mouth. She had learnt to gouge out the guts and gills; check for spots inside the belly; use the bones for broth; fill the hollow with lentils and green chillies, then sew it back shut. The blood hadn't bothered Luni as much as the movement of the sharp blade along the spine, which brought back the dirty thrill of the bait, a sensation that had made her say again and again for the beautiful tiles she'd see with her eyes tightly shut: *Now finish. Don't stop. Just finish it.*

And it had been strange at first to find those tiles arranged around town outside her body as squares or broken pieces fitted into mosaics, shimmering on the wall of a puncture shop or at the post office. The art of piecing them together, someone had told her, came from people who began sorting bits of porcelain jugs and saucers that were filled into ships to weigh down the bottom and later purged on the port as waste. Now to see those patterns painted on lampshades. Luni was amazed by the intricate eggs, the wild rooster, frogs along the border and the different shades of the sea she found everywhere. Somehow, the most beautiful tiles were in the unlikeliest places, like the wall of a grim public toilet, where she had stared at a single small square of red poppies. A trident of dark green topped with perfect disks so bloodshot, and a near smudge for a bud. Riveted, Luni had made up her mind to find a tile just like it or copy the design on cloth for her home.

She usually got all the fish she needed straight off the boats so the trip she made to the market sometimes on her days off from work was just to soak up the energy of the place in the morning and enjoy the company of the women. She'd wait for the bus to the main market, which never came on time and was always packed with men—swaying in the aisles, men in the laps of men. They chatted, dozed, munched, spoke on the phone or stared at their knuckles in astonishment, as if the seat of some old amphibious drive had suddenly revealed itself. A few familiar faces looked out the windows and regarded the road. The inevitability of it. It seemed to leap out of heads in power to cut through and climb over anything. No matter what the cost, or who got displaced in the process. No court order or sacred concern could halt it for too long. The tribes of the island knew this after little remained of them and their protest. To even stand a chance fighting, the priestess of the neighbourhood had told the men, one needed to try at the source, while it was still tentative. Stop it right there or at least keep it friendly. And so the men in the bus, sleeping or wide awake, did what the woman had prescribed as a regular exercise—dream of a rope and keep it straight. No knots, no curves, not even the slightest quivering. Luni could tell they were doing that by the restlessness beneath the lids and the sudden smacking of the thighs. She herself had tried but never succeeded and, after a few attempts, would find herself thinking of items to pick up on the way: sweet potatoes, incense, pyramids of jaggery ... Just a little something to hold—the groceries would be bought another time.

She'd walk to the very end of the main market and into the canopy, where the day's catch lay spread out on pointy stone counters before the women, who were an explosion of colour in their bright saris, blouses and floral nightgowns. Their voices loud because of the rim inside. Some of them made the extra effort of enhancing the display—adding shells to the counters, a necklace of fish or holding up a long, slender specimen with small cuts on both sides that made the flesh open up like a vine of pendulous flowers, false birds-of-paradise. Sometimes, small fights would erupt when a customer looked into one stall and bought from another, but the women always ate and sang together, signed petitions, scratched lottery tickets and fretted about the boats going further in. They sat among crates and threw their scraps to loitering kittens. Whistled to the men cleaning fish at the cutting slabs, where scales floated in the air like ice flakes. They used newspapers to lay their snoozing infants between bowls of shrimp and broke biscuits for the toddlers on their thighs. The stingray always saved for regular customers, partially covered with muslin. Funny-looking shovels, Luni had thought upon first seeing them. With googly eyes. The tail a thin line, like a glint of sun on the tools buried in sand the children loved to dig out, screaming and moaning about their hands. The women had told her that on certain days, especially around the monsoon fair, the funny-looking shovels could be happy-looking as well.

In fact, everything seemed more cheerful around the popular event. Even though the town had begun to receive spells of unusual rainfall throughout the year, the fair marked the arrival of some of the wettest months and the statewide fishing ban that was put in place to let the stocks recover. Tables would be set up in a public ground close to the market for vendors to sell all kinds of things—clothes, cosmetics, jewellery, teapots. The women of the neighbourhood brought their pickles, preserves, snacks and sweets. Luni helped them sort out jars, prepare both old recipes and exciting new ones: tangy prawns, ginger jam, stuffed raw mangoes, sweet-and-spicy eggplant. She carried a notebook to take down tips for her own kitchen and wiped the streaks of red that ran down the women's foreheads. Leaving no sample that came her way—sucking on new concentrated flavours that broke in waves against the walls of her cheeks, biting into altered skin, drinking the potent brine—Luni would make the mistake of enjoying too much too quickly, like the lurkers who came to taste everything on the tray but bought nothing, and twice, she'd suffered a nosebleed.

The kitchen rounds were rife with gossip and Luni enjoyed telling stories from work. This time, she chose the home appointment with a foreigner named Annie, whose platinum blonde hair had fallen out rapidly, leaving the shape of a nipple behind her head. Her face was pale, as though she nibbled clay, but kind enough. She had once offered Luni a pair of leggings she'd got tired of without ever wearing and would often save Himmo toys from her cereal boxes, saying all the little sugar animals tasted the same. She had learnt to swim in India, skip stones, fold paper into a neat hat before a boat. She had worked for the sprawling hotel on the beach for a little while and enthralled Luni by sharing odd and broken bits about it: the massive guard dog who answered to 'Juice' because that was how his keepers pronounced 'Zeus', the nervous manager who went around each night checking the height of chairs in the lobby, the four chocolate-covered cashews delivered in every room at four in the evening, the defunct rowing machine. But what Luni could never fathom was why she had chosen to get rid of her eyebrows. Was it right after the hotel gig? The waxed forehead, in tandem with the hair and skin, gave Annie the sort of look that unsettled people in the streets instead of eliciting straight adoration—they did not know whether to avert their eyes from the insane act or ask for a photograph. On top of that, the fallout. Luni felt sorry for her. Rubbing an onion on her client's scalp, she had tried pacifying the petrified body. *Baal hi toh hai, madam.* It is only hair.

The women gasped in thin horror, then giggled. They knew it was not just hair—every roadside barber knew that. Any trucker who had braids hanging from the front, side or back of his truck knew that a single strand could keep the edge willing. That's why some of the women even placed a stool, a comb and a tiny mirror outside their homes as a rest stop for the wild wind that passed through, heralding the rains. It was an offering so as to be spared from wreckage. A woman added that girls barely fifteen were losing their hair around town, but not in the neighbourhood. Luni nodded, tucking a lock behind her ear.

In another house, a woman peeling garlic told the story of a man in the north who'd bought his daughter a bulldozer decorated with garlands and big red balloons as a graduation present.

To secure her future, she said.

The woman grinding mustard seeds shook her head. The gift and the bulldozer stage for the skimpy lady in the latest item song was one thing, but what was a whole other class of insult was its presence in the playground. The yellow seat on the merry-go-round. How it had shrunk itself to pull all the venom out and make you want to do what it had done to you—break, kill, punch open, pull every nut out, smear, spill with music on. All so that the town could pin you down and drag you out and watch the children blame you too. Watch the children's dry eyes and their hands by their sides when it called you names other than human. And it took something extraordinary then, some barely breathing unhurt sense of self, to fight every impulse of the body, to keep the skirt down, the spit in the mouth and watch that thing thrill the playground.

Or one could find a way to do what she had done—snatch power away from the town in whatever little way possible. And she had done so with the aid of her own equipment: her washing machine. How she had flung herself over its off-white body when they came for the demolition, and now it was plugged in at a rented place. Two scoops of the powder with the with the double action of rose and jasmine, and the clothes came out flawless, fragrant and dry. She was still the only woman in the neighbourhood to own one. Bought from the money she'd got at her wedding, she had seldom used it for herself and her family, and now it served a more potent purpose.

There were the people she worked for, the good folks with the big home, who never missed an opportunity to educate—the names of ministers and the shapes of temples, the separation of different kinds of waste. They had told her about the large crowd that had assembled at the beach before the hotel ever came up, to bid farewell to a portion of the ashes of the Father of the Nation. How fourteen-year-olds had mouthed pledges to the cause of freedom that day, and mothers, stifling their own need to jump into the water, had not wiped their children's faces. The milkmen had boarded boats that rode close to the one carrying the urn and emptied their jugs and vessels right after the scattering, till the sea near the shore turned white, as though the man's own cloth that he pulled between his legs and draped around his waist and thighs had bloomed bloodless for the very last time. Then years later, the state commissioned a statue to mark the historic event and when the renowned sculptor ran out of material in the middle of his work, he melted the bust of his own father to build what some said, in recent times, were disproportionately long legs. Others argued that art couldn't be judged in that way, and hadn't similar comments about a poet somewhere succeeded in shifting his bust?

The people with the good home added to this story bit by bit—a procession through town with hymns and speeches; the police baffled by the size of the crowd. They swore to have donated money for the repair of the ground where the immense statue now stood, where many protests had been held in the good old days and which also hosted the monsoon fair. They claimed to have gone through their channels to try and stop the bulldozer, which she could not believe because no TV reporter, not even the usual one or two, had shown up for her round of demolition. It was these people—who had not given her the meagre *tch-tch-tch* before or after it was all gone, had even given her a day off to mourn—who did not have a washer. They believed in the luxury of getting their clothes hand-washed. And it worked out till the rain came pouring endlessly, and they found themselves haunted by the stink.

The entire house became a challenge to breathe in. Even the youngest, the most innocent of the lot, who slept beside a vase of beautiful peacock feathers, smelled like an open drain. They first thought it was something they ate, then found the fault in their damp clothes and tried the iron, and when it couldn't cope, they turned and asked her to purge their load in her personal machine.

And she did. She, who wondered what was drowning in all that talk, who swept their floors and washed their clothes but would not touch their food, not the big slice of cake put aside for her between two plates or even to experience the difference between snow and shaved ice. She took in their rude laundry, holding her head high and her breath in so that the face gave only liquid grace, and watched their lowered eyes. They knew this was her small, sweet revenge; that if she wanted, she could make a noise about it. They knew that she knew, after all the steps, the stench would remain. For its strength lay someplace else. In that curfewed place. And the stench of the rained-on was a homecoming.

It did not change her situation or take the edge off it, but at least when she pushed back to the rented place, holding the bag up close to the nose, taking in the stink, she could think of laying her head on the shaking machine at the end of the day, and walk past the playground.

Its arm came to bury the fish, said a woman writing ingredients on her palm. Anyone who touched that wretched thing could have tempted it.

—

The festivities around the fair lasted a few busy days as the residents hosted their own ceremonies and once, there had been a gathering to mark the birth of a mother whose child had arrived feet first. She sat on a plastic chair with a bundle in her arms, the boats lined up behind her. The women waved sparklers and blessed her baby, one of them kneeling down to gently coax the tiny fist into a wave, as if to declare the games open. Luni participated in sneakers and got handsomely teased for it. When the women broke into song, she listened intently to their words. *Jabilli*, the moon; *Bordoisila*, the wild wind spirit; *Fehu,* the colostrum of a cow. Words from their native towns and villages that moved like gumballs in her mouth. Words that breathed rest into the body and undid the violence of other words such as justice, precipice, island, and of questions such as *Where are you from? Why do you come to the sea to die?* Luni had savoured them and marvelled at the heft of her own tongue, hoping all the while that the springiness of a few remained in her mind for future use.

Then the priestess came. Among many things, she was known for dumping rotten fish on the magistrate's desk and somehow being spared for it. It warped the residents' entire understanding of punishment, considering the man who had clapped behind her had only invited an eviction notice. The priestess was a mystical being. All she could tell of her own birth was that it was afternoon and it had been raining. She could curse a thing back to life, just like her mother had done every day till the time they took her to the hospital, where she died, drowned in milk. Now the priestess carried on with the good work. She maintained that she had only presented the fish to the magistrate, not hurled or dumped it. Never mind that the man who had clapped behind her was one-armed.

The old woman, during the gathering, had hobbled to the sea and scooped the spume in a plastic mug, her coffee-coloured indie trotting behind her. Upon finding the mother looking straight ahead, she had nudged her face downwards, then flicked a few drops of water on the child's legs and led a prayer: *May you taste only till the knee and never turn away from her.*

The mother had tied around the baby's ankle a string of white rocks found in horned fish heads. The women showered petals of different colours and the baby, her hand back into a fist, heard the first promise that would be broken—the fugitive sigh of the rainbow.

Much later, the girl would push the jagged remainder of the very chair her mother had sat on and learn how to walk. She would also swallow a shoe whistle. She would fit between her parents and take off her ruby sock for the boy sitting opposite her, and when that boy, all grown, would turn around and call her a termite in front of her community, she'd smile. Smile broad when he'd repeat it, broader till he was gone. For she'd take the truth out of it—that was how she loved. His mighty talks about bird love, how far they could go, how high, but what she could do he could not even think of. People like her flew towards the light and when they landed to find each other, where they landed, they arched back. They twisted and turned their bodies, or caught their wings in objects and backed all the way, till each blade bent and broke. That was bug love. It was what people like him would always be afraid of—that they stay.

Luni had stayed back after the gathering and watched the waves rise and crash headlong onto the shore. If her turn came, she thought, it could come cool enough. She wouldn't have to yearn for some snowy peace anymore. This one could be cool and quick enough. But then to suddenly grasp the slight weight on her feet and feel a pang in the throat. The shoes, with their frayed tongues, could be counted upon to walk her briskly back home.

The night before the fair, when music blared in the neighbourhood, even the displaced danced along with the rest. The residents formed groups and the party moved from one house to the next. There were fireworks and good food. Drunk men sang and swayed; women put up yellow lights to mark their standing homes. They drew designs on the floor with rice flour, wore flowers and ribbons in their hair, put henna along their palm lines. They dressed in polyester saris, reversing for the day the important order of things, wearing light under their drapes and closer to the skin—baby blue petticoat under navy, seaweed over mint. Sweaty children struck poses like the crane they'd seen at the construction site.

The residents celebrated till the first drool of dawn, and only once they were back in their towers of silence did the churn return to the belly, hopped on by the mapmaker.

# 18

I SAW IT FIRST.

But I picked it first.

Like thumbs, Himmo and her friend wrestled over a sole. A soft light illuminated their faces as they pulled, pushed, whirled about.

It's mine, she said, grabbing his elbow. The flip-flop was beyond her reach in his other hand.

Get off! I picked it. I was going to say let's share again but you—

But *I* want to win this time.

You only want what the dice man has.

No. I also want to win.

The boy was astounded by her sharpness. So unexpected, like that kiss cut by the barbed wire of the PE teacher. Behind the office door, the air made tougher by the piece of spinach stuck like a ripped kite. Swept there by the promise of being chosen for the next match and the report card comment: *May his anthems be short.* Now tussling with Himmo, he wondered: Could dust be sharp as well?

He tried holding her off at first. When she didn't relent, he dragged her closer to the water. Himmo tried to pull him back, but he was much stronger. Soon, the sea was lapping at her ankles.

Give it up, he threatened. Or I'll pull you in deeper.

Fear flashed in Himmo's eyes and she kicked his legs. He lost balance and took her down with him just as a wave rushed in. She squealed as her clothes drank up water and her skin tasted salt, sand and the bristle of the line. Under the glare of a weak sun, a mere boy had made her cross it. Now what would she tell her mother? Could she uncross it? Her whole life reduced to a type. She tried to rise, but found herself fixed to the ground. Another wave was rolling in. What would she have to do? Divvy up the dunes with seashells? Wear rouge on her knees? There came no answer, but a bright round thing hit between her legs. Himmo picked it out of the water: a float from a fishing net. She scratched it a little and then, holding on firmly, got up, but wasn't steady enough when the boy grabbed her hair, yanked one of the loose pearls on her headband and tossed it into the water. Himmo stood still and watched the bead disappear completely. A bobbing took over, a bobbing that said the final wound would not be hers. She only had to get out of the way. She closed her eyes and nodded and when the power raced through her, with a soundless scream, she dropped the ball, lunged at the boy walking away and sank her teeth hard and deep into his forearm. He howled and chucked the rubber into the sea.

And then something caught the feed. Unknown to the two pairs of terrible human eyes on the beach, something that had been lingering close for a while bit the sole in the water and dragged it away.

# 19

ARTH'S KNEES BUCKLED THE FIRST time she wore the scuba tanks on her back. She was at a pool getting a crash course in diving basics after days of searching for the missing boy with the help of the police, the coast guard and paid specialists who were typically called in to free the silt. They had put posters all over town—in the main market, at bus stops and even inside the church of lost and found things, where a table was set up every Sunday for people could come and reclaim their items. Someone said a model of a ship called *Endurance* once hung from the rafters right above the table, but no one knew where it went. Yet there had been great successes and people had found on separate occasions a stock of canned cherries and a child in a helmet (who was later recruited as baby Jesus for the annual Nativity scene. Each kid in the choir had blown on top of a finger for a candle, save for one who had blown on two). Such was the usual desperation for keys, phones, wallets and handkerchiefs that only a few seemed to care that the god hoisted in front had not his head slumped downwards but looked alive and aching, and staring straight ahead. It was the passion of the chameleon, who, in the flashing moments, dons at once every costume only to rupture through them all. Christ's brown body fleshier; the legs kept side by side. The boy's mother had spent a long morning staring back at this god, asking if on her son's plate that day, she had served the plums stoned-in. Yes, she had, she had.

Then, while Arth pinned the poster on the message board next to a survey announcing WHO'D YOU RATHER PRAY WITH?, she had walked to the table and picked up a cotton-candy maker that could turn the hardest lozenge into cloud. And now she wanted to implore the water.

She had been advised to do so in an email by a kind member of the Committee of Parents of the Disappeared, whose first automated response included the message: *Is your child having trouble blinking? Call 1-800-ESCAPE.*

But there was no place Arth could go as she crumpled on the pool's edge. Her mind focused sharply on her stomach. Trapped fat; rolls of Richter grease. The instructor helped her up. She recalled how disoriented she had been during her first casual swim in the sea, struggling against the sparseness, for the community pool in the country's capital where she grew up had never not been congested. Children thrashing across the breadth of the pool as adults chased lengths, making a backstroke simply unfeasible. The girls who dropped their skirts right at the edge, testing the water with their feet, which the boys, to get noticed, pulled all the way in. The row of ladies in animal print parked at the shallow end, watching the little risks and accidents. Only one among them dipped her head in and out of the water. She wore a giraffe-print swimsuit with a matching cap, and big, orange bands wrapped around her arms. Arth remembered her most distinctly. Could tell back then she felt brave while dipping. Liked to think of her as brave. Liked to ignore the incompetence of the body amplified by the water wings. An extra-large version of a child's swimmies. Could larger water fix it—the shameful look of it? Arth had wondered this as she slipped into the sea and soon enough, felt herself fumbling.

We'll try again, the instructor said.

Three days later, zipped in wetsuits, five of them—Arth, the artist, the boy's mother and two instructors—were on a boat. The artist's gaze was fixed on Arth.

You don't have to do it, you know, the mother said to her.

No, no, Arth stammered. I'm fine.

Your breathing is shallow. I will go because he is my son.

They descended at a location not too deep, three of them guided closely by the instructors. Arth bit hard on her regulator. She kept telling herself to breathe through the mouth. Her brain, unable to register where she was or what she was seeing, fell back on its previous stance: that there was nothing to be found—no fish, no sky, no boy, nothing. The instructor had advised her to think positive thoughts. On land, she had rehearsed a few options: hollyhocks swaying tall on a traffic island or the little mischief-maker on the plane who had climbed up on her seat and quietly opened the tray tables of the three men snoring behind her. No. Arth was locked out of the plane, and in place of hollyhocks, there were black buckle-shoes of little schoolboys drying on barren bushes. She needed something else to stick. But such things do not happen on command and instead, a sound pervaded her. A frenzied clattering of bills.

She looked at the boy's mother drifting ahead. There was no boy. The visibility wasn't great. Arth regretted her decision. She should have stayed up on the boat and supported the woman. After all, what did she know about her or her son? The search party had already done several sweeps. There was no boy, nothing. She'd known from the start that it was a senseless idea, yet it hadn't felt like a choice. Now all that Arth had poured out to the chalky ones came zooming back into her. She was bolting down a slope, out of control, when all of a sudden, the clattering eased. The instructor's hand was firm on her shoulder. Stop. Breathe. Arth slowed down and became aware of an elasticity holding her.

By the time they surfaced, the sky had grown darker. There was a chill in the air. Arth removed her flippers on the boat and felt her body cave in as she let out what sounded like a whale call. A whale snapped in half. Whale slapped on a billboard saying SENSITIVITY RELIEF AND NATURAL WHITENESS I GOT BOTH. Whale opened to reveal a greenhouse: four flowerpots, three hosepipes, thick plastic sheets, a plastic spray can, a window, ten metres of rope, a mattress, a pair of sweatpants and a few dozen plastic bags. There she bloats! The boy's mother stroked Arth's back, who then chuckled. She was reminded of her grandfather, who, in this situation, would have brought up something odd to make her feel better: *Did he have any detergent variety?* She'd answer, *Yes, one, with a label on it that said 'Please don't sprinkle on your roof. What do you expect will happen when it rains?'*

His oval face haggling unnecessarily with vegetable sellers next to the strange installation of cars stacked up high as if on a barbecue skewer or under the bright amaltas. C*assia fistula*. The scientific name of the yellow tree always made Arth cringe. It pulled up images of women leaking in tea gardens, oozing all that they were pregnant with—debris, dispersals, monstrosity; didn't storks do the same thing? Paint the legs with their own liquids to keep cool and sane. The women made public puddles, dishwater slips. One could toss a coin in. Tails and it's wheat. A man will plunge for it.

Her grandfather, whose thin hair she had oiled every Sunday, whose ashes she had rubbed all over her body, along with the unburnt bone bits, who had died with the unfulfilled wish of touching the sea just once.

As the boat swayed over the waves, the missing boy's mother began to speak.

It's clear. If someone's taken him, it's a case of mistaken identity.

No one questioned her.

He'll be back either way, she said, sounding weary. He's done it before, running off from his playschool when he was barely three.

She closed her eyes. It was Arth's turn to stroke her.

I was eight months in with his sister. Went to every shop looking for him. Finally, he showed up at the house late at night, so happy, with a red beacon on his head.

Red beacon? the artist said. Aren't they—?

This was before they banned it. He went all the way up to the field. Said the guard there was busy practising his secret voice, so he just plucked one. Said he could make it spin.

She leaned over the edge of the boat and extended her arm towards the water—dreaming octopus skin.

Come home, my love, she said with a quiver in her voice.

Then sternly. The rains will be here soon. Come home now.

# 20

LUNI REACHED HOME, FANNING her face with a magazine, and found two nervous children and a furious mother waiting for her.

She bit him!

Luni staggered back from the impact. The boy's bandage shone as the woman hurtled on about what had happened—a simplified tale told to her by her son: the two had been playing when a loose pearl fell from Himmo's headband and she bit out of anger.

Covering her face, Himmo began to whimper. The boy tried to wriggle out of his mother's grip and move towards his friend.

Without a word, Luni opened the door and dropped her bags and magazine on the floor. She walked to the kitchen area in silence, found a coconut and held it on the slab with one hand. With the other, she picked up a grinding stone.

Open your mouth, Himani, she said, with her back turned to them.

He pulled me into the water!

So? You'll bite? the boy's mother shouted.

We were just playing, the boy said.

I said open your mouth.

I'm sorry! He pulled my—

With a high and monstrous swing of her arm, Luni whacked the shell. Himmo screamed and covered her ears.

Open your mouth.

Himmo began to sob. Luni swung around.

Not a single tear, she roared.

Himmo pressed her hands against her mouth. The woman pulled her son closer to the door. When Himmo couldn't stop crying, Luni turned and struck again. She kept pounding the pieces.

Finally, the boy's mother intervened. Okay, that's enough. Leave it. Give the girl some water.

She grabbed her son's unwounded arm and led him home.

Later that night, Himmo did not eat her dinner properly. She lay on the bed facing away from her mother, whose cruelty in front of an audience had shocked her. She had anticipated a private beating, but the sound of the coconut splitting open and the sweet water spilling in vain had been too much to bear. And no emphasis on the boy's crime. Who knew how far he could have pulled her? No. All the blame was hers. They had honed in on the bite, but teeth, once trained, had their own mind. Her mother knew this; it was clear from the way her mouth hunted the most phenomenal chew. She could just stand there, working on the softest food or rolling her tongue on her teeth for the invisible seed. And the neighbourhood women had also preached not to be dainty with it. *Kadicha*, kadicha, they said, come on. They had taught her that and then betrayed her. Now only a wrong thing could respond to their wrongness, and Himmo thought of destroying the headband for a good while until her mother curved around her and gently kneaded her stomach, and the thought began to fade behind her shuttered eyes.

Waiting for her daughter to settle down, Luni scanned the room. The hand-stitched curtains and tasselled pillow covers, the banner made of fabric scraps that hung on the wall. But no clock. She'd got rid of them all. The last one had been a freebie from election season, and she'd ripped out its batteries and handed the body to the woman next door, who already had seven of them. Seven ticking faces! But not one was worth tolerating to Luni, not since they'd jailed a man for repairing the big clock on the tower. When they'd marched him out, there had been no handcuffs—just men holding hands. Luni liked to imagine those chains hanging from the roofs of police stations in a long desire for rain.

That dead clock's first shudder had wedged a fish bone in her daughter's throat, despite the careful morsels. Her gingerly shaped hills. How she had run out like a mad dog, rendered groundless by her tricks. Surely a result of all the times she'd thumped the earth for Himmo's bad falls. Fortunately, rescue had come in time in the form of a banana.

Luni patted her daughter and quietly pulled down the hem of Himmo's dress that had slid up her warm skin. She felt uneasy but convinced of the necessity of her actions. She had noticed worrying signs before—holding up clay pots, then letting them go; the poor indie caught and groomed with hot candle wax. Some of it she could do nothing about, like when peacocks sang silver along with Himmo's joyful voice: *nani teri morni ko mor le gaye baaki jo bacha tha kaale chor le gaye nani teri morni ko ...*

Himmo stirred. Luni detected something stinging the air and recognized it at once: her daughter's three-fold rain. She had to save all of it to fight the crumbs. Maybe even do more. She thought of her embroidery and considered adding Vs to the sky. What could the birds bring first? Even if with stiff flaps. Maybe rubber bands; maybe the smell of sleds.

# 21

FRIDAYS ALLOWED GUL A LONGER break at work, so she invited a student for lunch in her office. He was one of those enamoured with her and when he saw her sitting and reading on the sofa, her long braid not as a nest around her neck but wandering aimlessly, her legs up and folded to the side so that slivers of bare feet were visible like sweet little tantrums of flesh, he found himself rooted at the threshold. Gul looked at him and smiled.

Come in, she said.

She moved to her desk, shifting the braid to the front of her shoulder, while the young man searched his bag and took out a dark lump of rock to present to her.

You didn't have to—oh!

Mid-ocean ridge basalt: a piece of the seafloor. In a moment, the plates could shift apart and the molten magma rise to form new crust, but Gul kept that vision for time alone when she could really enjoy the spreading, perhaps even float in the fact that somewhere deep down at the bottom, there was a line of perfectly spaced holes. Man-made? Animal-made? Toying with the lump in her hand, she turned to place it on a shelf behind her chair, among the other rocks and minerals: malachite, pyrite, polished agate, mica schist, pumice. Most of them she pointed out as gifts from other professors and students. The curtains sighed on the open windows as she tipped the bubble in the quartz. The student noticed the textbooks and stack of red envelopes in the bookcase below.

Gul loved the oddest piece of rock more than any jewellery she owned, and while she could appreciate the craftsmanship of the dragonfly brooch, the zodiac pendants and most other designs, what pierced her were the poor little hounds: the opal dog with diamond eyes, the jasper dog with emerald eyes, the white chalcedony dog with cabochon ruby eyes. And she couldn't really tell why they pained her; perhaps it had something to do with sipping from some river that gave them those upwards-gazing human eyes.

Tell me, she said, turning around. If a tsunami without a triggering earthquake is an orphan tsunami, then what is an earthquake without an earthquake?

They tossed guesses as they ate, when in fact, both knew the answer but neither would say it. The student picked out an angel from his bed of white rice. How they beckoned with their arms open, those bruised cloves. How they fell for the mortar. Gul brought up a study on rainfed seismicity in a region further north on the coast that linked several consecutive low-intensity tremors to the percolation of water at a certain depth and the resultant collapse of underground cavities.

The challenge lies in assuring the villagers that there may not be a big one, she said.

The young man nodded. To handle the public pressure for information, to neither panic nor mislead, to stay in the ambiguous zone of 'unlikely but the possibility cannot be excluded' was a task he was not yet trained for nor too eager to deal with. Especially after the ordeal of the scientists abroad who were charged with manslaughter for inadequate warning before a disastrous quake, and who, even after their acquittal, had to face an angry crowd shouting, For shame! For shame! Piss on your predictions! The chanting really stoked doubt in his ambition. He wanted to do remarkable science and stick to just that.

Talking of seasonal occurrences, they soon hit storms and the student revealed his fascination with cyclones. How he looked forward to the names each year—Laila, Rosita, Yvette, Hudhud—as though they were pretty exchange students at a party. His collage of different cloud formations at the edge of storms. How he religiously tracked low-pressure systems in the North Indian Ocean, at times even wishing that those along the country's west coast intensified.

There was quiet after that, as the student reflected on how perverse the last bit may have sounded given the death and devastation sprayed across the region over the past few years. Wiping his mouth, he admitted to frequent bouts of confusion, his clogged ears. His fear of losing hearing altogether. There were days, he said, when he couldn't get up because life seemed like trudging through a dark and foetid lake.

But in the cyclone season, life whoops.

Gul nodded. That bad weather thrilled men and could even save them was not a revelation to her; she understood the power of the spell breaking. The dangerous buoyancy; a jolt out of the festering. Otherwise, one could stay a corsage of fake flowers anting through spring. And the boy's embarrassment was such a classic case. She wanted to say they're short-term losses but thought better of it. Tried another way.

We do a lot for the looker's comfort, she said, leaning forward. Paint our nails, lick dew, say the condition is inherited, call it Camp Grateful or Camp Love, but all those things reveal themselves. In any case, they know. They've known it all along. The flourish in a season's fade is a blind man's sermon, and we've all heard it. Lucky for you that the wells come up.

Her eyes roamed to the stapler on her desk, then back to him.

Better than shooting at hurricanes, isn't it?

His lips twitched into a smile. Gul's eyes lingered on his veins. Three parallel lines, like a bayleaf. Easy enough to memorize. She'd find that beautiful hand poking out of anyplace, and she'd hold it all day, all through the night.

But he could never know about the shaking.

# 22

Himmo sat with one leg folded and pressed under the other thigh in front of a black Buddha fountain close to the cashier. She waited for the numbness to set in, then stood up on the cold floor, enjoying the sensation creeping back into her flesh. Her mother had dragged her to the parlour as continuing punishment for the biting incident. There were two customers in the shop. Luni attended to a girthy being, wiping colour stains off her ears and forehead with a cotton ball. Each section of her hair had been meticulously painted—first mid-length, then roots, then ends—and placed on top in a pile. Another beautician worked on bleaching her client's face. A spindly, underage worker swept the floor. Her movements reminded Himmo of the women who stooped to sweep the sides of the tar mixture as it was poured in a strip on the main road.

The television played on mute and a celebrated astrologer beamed through, picking cards for different horoscopes. The cashier had turned on the radio for some Bollywood music on an overcast day.

Buddha couldn't weep, so the fountain was a stagnant pool. Himmo had spent some time spreading her palms on his face and massaging his earlobes. She fished out a few crumpled flowers from her dress pocket—treasures from the last standing plumeria near the construction site. Hung from its branches was a mass of white water cans over a shrine built by the fishermen. A small red structure decorated with bells, lace and ribbons; its crevices filled with shiny pebbles, and wishes written on chits and shells. It was home to stuffed toys and a row of idols, including Mary Mata in a sari, with a crescent at her feet atop a lotus base. She stood bowing next to a cross that curled, both covered with a mosquito net. Himmo, during her visits, would be mildly interested in her because of the unusual veil. She was 'their god wearing our clothes'. Himmo wondered what would happen if she changed the clothes and added a bit of makeup, but even then, in her mind, the face was kind and almost too sweet. Who really grabbed her was the little wooden man on the far right, put there by the priestess.

I told the junk shop guy exactly what I didn't want, the old woman had said. No beard and not blue, no crown or pets or nails or anything loud like that. But a turban with a little feather in it, now that could work. Red clothing and a moustache. A lovely, long moustache.

Himmo had looked at his eyes painted closed, the barely arched eyebrows and a mouth that was a red dash. The face worked as a face before a real face. It could switch at any time. The eyes could open and shoot flames; the mouth show teeth. Even if it was a smile, it would be something wide and powerful, not sweet. God in her mind could never just be sweet.

So you pray to him? she'd asked the priestess.

No, never.

Give him something?

No.

Then what?

Then nothing. We do nothing. The old woman pointed at his chest. See the necklace he's wearing?

Yes.

Could be pearls or skulls, you never know.

The uncertainty burst over Himmo like a cool pill and the knowing priestess watched eagerly. Such an even coating. Here was a follower whose deep wasn't deep enough yet, but her search was dark and deeper. She would test him. Soon she would be the coal he'd walk on. To seal the effect, the priestess told the girl what the junk dealer had told her: that this man could fly.

But he has no wings, Himmo said. And such small hands.

The old woman smiled. Now isn't that the best part?

Himmo smoothed each white petal on her thigh, then carefully placed the blossoms in a circle in the pool. Her forefinger made gentle ripples while her mind drifted to the sea that got caught in her clothes the day of the fight. She couldn't get it out of her head. And since she couldn't attach it to anything else, she lent it to the strong embrace of a father she knew very little about and couldn't remember much of, except for a shape frantically scribbling on the walls, and that too could be something she had made up. She wanted a father—old or new. It wouldn't matter if just the front two teeth at the top were really white and the rest of his smile yellow, or if he swallowed live fish that swam past the scum of his voice. He would love her and hold her hand, and they would frolick in the sea; he would buy her a new dress and dates and a sharpener and pinwheels and pearls for her headband. She wanted him with a shiny belt buckle. His presence would be a glimmer she owned, like an inside organ, so that when she walked in the dark, she looked like starlight from the back and shorelights from the front. The line would not hurt her.

Whenever Himmo asked her mother about him under the guise of wanting a last name, she got a terse answer: the cattle had died one bad summer, and he had died with them. But she felt, somehow, that wasn't true. That it was something regarding her that had made her mother leave. And it was a good thing that she only felt this way, for had the black blot lifted and allowed remembrances from her earliest days—from the first shiver out of mother-water that had deemed her good enough for sacrifice, to the raised hand—chances were she would have believed it. Her father's silver drip falling too close to her mouth while her mother knelt holding her was unspeakable enough to not look any further. But that wasn't it. In fact, it was the other thing in the lap at another time—that orphaned flesh of fawn biting the bullet-sweating milk. It was Luni's fingers in its soft fur; the lilac breath making the flakes of dried skin flutter; the warm, untainted animal suck that had singlehandedly outweighed her existence on the other nipple and granted her mother a rush of more than love—a wish of total abandonment. Luni had fled to save herself for her daughter.

In any case, the blot was lodged steady in its place and Himmo's insistence for a father went so far as to suggest fasting for the name, which caused Luni to lose control and slap her hard across the face.

You want to go hungry, do you? Hungry by choice? My name for you isn't full enough? Go on then, call yourself twice. Tell your teacher that.

Himmo had earnestly tried, but it sounded fake, like the second time wasn't a bell but its tape recording. The result, perhaps, of ringing too loudly. How on earth could the first name be her last name.

She looked over her shoulder and saw Luni trying to sell something. Her mother called it pretty work, but she sounded unpleasant and servile. The way she hovered even after being refused, hoping to sell some other service.

Get half-legs done, madam. I'll do it quickly while we wait. Your just sip your tea and relax.

Himmo turned away. She watched the water wimpling.

A few minutes later, there was a new arrival in the parlour. A woman draped in light yellow; her thick, unbound hair covering her chest; her toes adorned with silver rings. The clouds growled behind her as she walked in. Luni looked at the woman and frowned.

I told you to come later, she said.

I couldn't wait, the woman replied. She spotted Himmo near the fountain and patted her head.

Five pearls are missing, she said and managed a smile.

Himmo knew her. She was her mother's friend from the neighbourhood. Luni hurried over to the woman and nudged her close.

Did you speak to the guy who sells it as stuffing?

The woman nodded.

The cashier, fair and scalded, who also owned the shop, signalled for them to meet at the sinks. After a short exchange, they emerged and the owner called out to the sweeper.

Get my blade.

Luni's customer grasped what was happening and watched with wild eyes as the woman in yellow took the seat closest to Himmo.

Are you sure you want to do this? Luni asked, her face creased with worry.

Yes.

All of it?

All of it.

There was no time to call an Ammonia, and the matter was much too sacred in any case.

The woman turned to Himmo. You look at your flowers, okay?

Himmo nodded. Bobcut, she whispered. Feather cut.

The clouds got louder; the love song made no sense. Himmo looked up. Her body could feel the tension in the room. The owner had turned the chair around, away from the mirror, and was pushing the woman's head down to get a closer look at the crown. Her razor angled near the scalp, the blade keen for carnage. Others in the parlour watched motionless, so furred and furled with terror that the sweeper suggested latching the door, and she had barely turned to do so, when, in the final moments before contact, with a loud boom, the sky broke.

They rushed to push open the door. Himmo with her mother; the customer with bleach on her face following close. The sweeper, upon that first scent of rain, began murmuring under her breath: *Saapan Mori, Bhoot vali Mori ...*

The owner stepped out but did not get wet till the razor dropped. Himmo watched it spin and cut the earth to let the white shoots sprout—the mouth letting out all the swords it had swallowed.

# Glass Bottom

after Primo Levi

This covenant of hunger
the bruised gem calls feather;
the warm mud keeps for the gopher keel,
and it brings forth the leviathan.
She comes from the dragged mares' thump,
the fragrant reef of half-widows and widows-
to-be. He drew them out
of grief and pride, but forgot the stirrups.
The stirrupless drove him mad.
A white sock and a back unbroken—
what wild passion is her foil?

The women on the beach make a see-saw
and a letter. Nine folded, bone after bone;

and a belly swollen fulcrum. Pass, pass, pretty.
How she mimics the grime.
She eats near the trough of light:
her worship and her penance.
Sweet for the sizes, so bloody
for the fire that won't keep.
Then what lascar's gold
fret tempers the crime and sets alight
the gusset tongue that proffers her to Him?
The great god, the latex lord of dust
and misgivings.

His hair mumbling ship
breaker; his name a hot-hawked howl.
But the see-saw wants the girl
named Seahorse. The boy named Breeze to bring music
for the sweetlips. And if he sips,
she will thoroughly seethe
*How much did you hear?*
*That her anchors were never used. The enormous white*
*forged in a landlocked country—*

And when it splits, she will heave
and cling to that stoneless ring

## GLASS BOTTOM

*I will birth a daughter and raise a lover*
*I will birth a daughter and tase a son—*

Lo, a glass bottom.
She will grind down her teeth
for the baptism.

But such a bloody thing is she
beyond the sad gallop:
Penelope of this merry-go-round
left seven skirts up
and seven stars wide,
a thick throb for the crest
fallen black wood and slide;
tender for the fisherman's boat
in the east, the last boat
of blind fantasy.

The future's fee is the lullaby
turning. The seat is wet.
Now who will ride
on her.

# II

# 23

IT WASN'T LONG BEFORE NEWS of the first storm began to arrive, and Arth wanted to know its name.

Sangai, Gul said. It is likely to move north-northwestwards and reach Gujarat.

Sangai? As in the deer?

She nodded.

They were sitting in the veranda on a salvaged school bench, a gift from the artist who had bolted it down. Scratched into the back were calculations: A+J J+J K=I. Arth was particularly pleased by the wicked equal sign and liked to imagine it as the instruction of some deary who wore rings on all fingers, each a different flavour of Fun Flips. If you carved it out well, she'd let you have tomato straight off her hand.

Gul sat on one end of the seat, stroking her knee. Arth sat on the other end, looking at the garden and occasionally glancing at her mother, who was savouring a fat slab of imported chocolate. It was her grandfather's birthday, and the two of them had just finished planting a sapling in his memory. They hadn't spoken much since their stop on the way home from the nursery, caused by a single palm leaf that lay flinching on the road—a local's way to halt traffic. Arth had stretched her head outside the car's window and watched as a man on top of a tree dropped coconuts. Their *thud thud thud* entered the vehicle and moved past silences to confront the strain accumulating for years.

There was no clear demarcation as to when it started, but it was roughly around the time Arth took over as the Scrabble champion of the house, carefully avoiding her mother's club of players who bore down on words with their prefixes and suffixes, and made MAN into MANOR or MANHOLE, CORE into SCORE, but not BOW into CROSSBOW. No, that was unacceptable. That would be doing too much and taking it too far. Arth agreed that language must not be tested this way. It can boast and buck on a whim. *Like free speech? Here's a sticker!* Language alone can taste the extra hour.

Occassionally, Arth would borrow the move, if only to antagonize her mother, and make works such as BLACKGANG and COCKTHROWING.

That's not a word, Gul would say.

It sure is.

Why can't you play normally? What is it? Some kind of mating dance?

Too ugly for that.

Use it in a sentence.

*The boys were cockthrowing all summer.*

Oh my god.

*The mother's busted boilers—*

I don't want to play anymore.

The games came to an end once tensions exacerbated with the death of her grandfather. One day in Delhi, he had spat out red, saying it was a petal of the gulmohar tree. Then came the slow days of hospital visits and the old ways to the Beating Retreat. Beating, beating, beating retreat. Talking many times about the decked-out camels, for the swaying, colourful beauties alone made the parade worth watching. Guessing which year it was when they started wearing the long yellow tassels down their chins and the golden neckbraces. Closer to the hospital, a different game played: Could be a hairpin in the lung or just a trim inside. Could be a disguise. And would it matter much, if a bird with one good lung could still make music? They had carried on this way till the day he turned to the doctor and said, Can you hear it?

Hear what? Arth said.

Put those things in your ear, It's my ribs.

The doctor's face had hardened, and Gul had snatched his stethoscope to have a listen. When she gasped, Arth decided to hear it too, and she could have reckoned with a whistle, a creaking sound, even really bad violin, but what came through was the clear end of a song, the exhortation of a man wearing a red nose and dungarees, waving his hands at his audience. *Jaiyega nahin, mera tamasha khatam nahin hua, joker ka tamasha khatam nahin hua, jaiyega nahin, jaiyega nahin ...*

Oh what a wonderful city of the deranged lung. Soon, her grandfather had got sick of tubes and wanted no new treatments—a decision Gul seemed to easily accept. To Arth, it had felt like giving up, as if Gul's own exhaustion had swayed her. She never quite understood it. That the lofty act of letting go exceeds what is lost—was that it? The mother and daughter had not discussed it in the aftermath, save for that one time in the early days, when even the faintest cobweb seemed capable of slitting a swimmer's neck. Arth had burst into Gul's room and accused her of not fighting enough.

I did, Gul said calmly, gazing out the window of her apartment.

You did not. You just let him quit.

He knew what he wanted.

There could have been a miracle.

Stop with the English movies.

You stopped! Was it too hard? Was it the money? No wonder you hid our—

Gul swerved around. Fight for what? And who do you think you are to decide that?

With swollen eyes, Arth had stared at the space above the side table, her pain taking shape around the pause, much like a snow globe—something she would later shake from time to time in the hope of finding a new answer. Gul turned back to the window. Say what really hurts, she muttered.

What do you mean? We abandoned him. What else can really hurt?

Okay.

No, say it!

Don't push me.

Say it!

That in the end, the only name he called was mine. Gul, Gul. Gulmohar. You too were Gulmohar, and when he did manage to say your name once, he split you in half.

The words travelled through Arth like a wave down a rattle. It was true; a deep, labouring breath and then *Ardh*. He had struck her right down the middle.

It had taken some seasons and an episode of running away from home for Arth to realize that the only way to survive the hurt was forgiveness. Forgive the two of them without working on the specifics. Hadn't he done that again and again? The way he'd justify each news of jumping by bringing up the incident with the eagle when he had been up on the roof fixing the antenna. Arth had been too young when it happened.

If I had tumbled, he'd said, you and your mother would have thought I ended it. You would have searched through all my sadness and found your own. But it was the white whorl on the back of my head that caught the bird's eye and when it attacked, I almost lost balance. Maybe something similar happened to the boy from the other block, maybe it was the monkeys. They'll push you right off. They'll snatch your shirt and go sit somewhere high and then, looking straight at you, pull out the buttons one by one. Such cruel things. Haven't you heard, they're now stealing from blood banks.

Arth had wanted to remind him that the boy had plummeted at night, when monkeys usually sleep, but she was so spooked by the mention of the eagle and so grateful that he was still alive that she let it be. In his denial, she chose to see forgiveness. And now that he was gone, she needed help. She needed to learn more about the act and knew exactly who could teach her. Keeping with the rib music and a little bit of *dit-dit-tiddle-diddle-dit-tit-ta-ra dit dit tiddle-diddle-dit-tit-ta-ra*, Smiley and Copycat.

At the camps, with their sideshow, the two bowing and spilling for the guards.

They have come to their present roles after deeply pondering the question: If everybody in the world wants to play a fool, then what is the fool good for? Smiley stretches seductively like a reclining lady; Copycat paints him. Then Copycat flogs a sack of potatoes, while Smiley hides in a sack down the line. Smiley is heavier with the part that seeks forgiveness. He started young after seeing a face out of a bus window, a little shining clown face made up with just a handful of dust and some tears. The large, dimpled smile that lifted up the cheeks when he waved. That unforgettable smile. She was begging; and since he, the boy she was calling to, sat higher up, she cupped her palm and, keeping her elbows straight, moved her arm up and down, up and down. To him, who gazed at her while searching his pockets for some change, it seemed that she alone had the power to hoist the sun and set it. Make it rise again; set it deeper down. The light from the sky flickered around her. He did not end up giving her anything that day, but only because he was ashamed that what he had to give was too little.

Copycat, on the other hand, is taller. He whips with conviction. Struggles to forgive even when the wronged has. *It's the same trick done twice a day, seven days a week for fifty years. There are no bad days, no bad waves. Just speed runs, explosions, back breaches, splashes, slide outs, high jumps, the world rides on the belly, the world rides on the back. Kiss kiss. Forgiveness comes at you from three sections, then dies.* Sadness fills Copycat's eyes. *Total forgiveness is a dream in clicks. Only Lolita could have taught you that.*

But Arth was split in half, and she had to remedy that somehow—sew back the parts even if loosely; so the two clowns bow and point to the corpse she and her mother had washed together. First, with soap and water: holding his head up so the liquid didn't run back into his ears, pressing his stomach lightly to expel any waste. Then working the curd mixture as if across the floor of a temple. On his chest, arms, in his armpits, belly button, on his thighs. Arth had looked away while Gul quickly washed the penis. Then his hips and knees, and the murky toenail that had pulled the string of the cloth fan above his granddaughter's crib during long power cuts. Arth had rinsed, clipped and filed it into shape before bathing him again with turmeric water, tying the two big toes together and dressing him for the crematorium.

The workers there had brought out a stock of mango wood, and Arth had felt the bile rise in her throat. It was then that she heard the juggler for the first time, after one of the loaders explained how they had to source the wood from another village because the usual one had run short, and it was not because there were too many people lying down or the trees being cut for other reasons; but because the farmers chose it, or it was chosen for the daughters—the holy wood unholied by the noose. Arth had thought about the father who could not cut his daughter down before the procedure of the police, so he quietly wiped her toes with the edge of his kurta and smiled at the smiling children who crunched on candies meant for sucking. Those little ones born into the old but exciting play, the ventriloquy of an active night, passive night. For whom a man on fire was yet another treat for the eyes—a festive feature. A bonus thrill if the burning man shot back flames. Those children were unafraid under the tree, for they'd seen a dozen scarecrows and believed that the nose would grow an inch longer, as it also did in stone. And that extra inch would store jewels. See the black papaya pearl barely escaped from her nostril? The father had touched their heads and no one in the crowd had cried—except for maybe a howl or two. There was no question of pollution. People just stood or sat close to the bodies hanging from the tree, waiting, waiting, waiting for it to come back—that deep-down longing for something sticky and sweet.

Arth had felt the back of her neck erupt because of the legs. Legs in sequinned orange and purple salwars, in loose white pants. Legs that were swept away only when her grandfather came out, swathed in the ocean of his wife's saris: gold-green, aquamarine, homage blue. The workers there had their own collective term for bodies: a washing.

She had wanted to save the turmeric water, but her mother's refusal had been bitter and hard. She had slept in his room before a week was up. The only room in the house where three-fourths of each wall was painted blue from the bottom, and at the top was a band of heavenly white. In that blue, the waves were always bigger. Big and hollow. They broke like no other. Quietly broke. When he was gone, she lay on his side of the bed, like a tusk, sailing.

Now searching for a grip, Arth recalled his lucidity that had absorbed all curiosity for his wife. What little she knew about her grandmother she had received without an appetite. For instance, how once, after bathing in a river she and her friends had looked for stones to scrape their feet. Then little cries in the air when the stones turned out to be turtles. The speckled quality of these stories made Arth think of a large, golden fish so strong from swimming upstream, being hauled out for photographs. A few remarkable poses, then let back into the pure, swelling world of symbols.

He was more concrete. Had left behind his chalk collection in a lunchbox. Those long, pale sticks barely used and saved for special occasions, whose existence as mere stubs in his hands had been an overwhelming thought. She recalled how, on his last day, he had exhumed his teaching voice:

*Can everyone hear me in the back? Vani?*
*What did the sightseer see?*
*Whose legs?*

*What kind of cash crop?*
*What did he write back home?*
*Yes, a memorial.*
*What sound does memory make?*
*Like water rushing down a burn scar.*
*Shhhhhhh … shhhhhhhh*

How language bucks. *We baptize you in the name of the Father, of the Son and of the Holy Spirit. Pew pew pew.* Say it fast and then say it twice. Steals back from a stolen church.

Arth looked at her mother and saw the brown film on the sides of her lips. She inhaled sharply to expel the familiar revulsion that crept up whenever Gul rejected her own garnishes or sat down with unrivalled softness and attention to oil her stones, as though they were vestiges of her unborn children. The milk could be boiling over or it could be Arth writhing in pain. Once, in the middle of the process, Gul had got up and, instead of a hot-water bottle, fetched her daughter a stick.

What am I supposed to do with this? Arth had yelled. Stab myself or beat the lump out?

Occasionally, the disgust would show on Arth's face in public, such as when Gul had dissected her sixth or seventh birthday cake, which she had painstakingly baked herself, only to demonstrate some tectonic activity even before the candles could be blown out. Or when the sweep of Gul's dress had shattered glasses off a table at a party, after which she calmly said *khatam ho gaye*. As though her father had been a packet of salt.

Hate can be resourceful, Arth reminded herself, like for doctors during war.

The paint on the bench was withering. Arth was wearing her grandfather's watch and its strap felt tight around her wrist. The minute hand moved in circles, but the hour hand had long stopped. *Sangai*, she thought, what an odd and gentle name for a cyclone. A deer of a plagued lake that dances across floating masses in the distant northeast, its only home in the world. A creature known to pause, even in flight, and look back—at what? Whatever makes it deer? Leaving behind or hoping for what to catch up? Then Arth saw it: a storm breathing like an animal in waiting. The name touching not what it is but what it loves, what arrives or not with the next day's sky.

Sangai, Arth enunciated slowly. An undulating name that fleetingly stirred her resolve to remain childless, made the day she'd seen the translator at an event cross his legs so that his shined shoe exposed all the nasty accretions of the sole—bits of tar, a thumb tack, puke and rubble—and touched the foreign novelist. *She writes better when she's ovulating.*

Time to sage quotations when the move burns all night long. She'd find the muse in mellow cud. Sangai. Such a pretty name for a girl.

# 24

A GROUP OF GIRLS IN the neighbourhood were finding out about Paris when the brigade came marching in. Huddled on a cot outside, they'd watched a video of a cock falling backwards from the force of his own crow and then switched to a clip about lambing season. How, after a lamb dies, its skin is wrapped around an orphan so that the mother takes to it. Then a streak of red dashed out and the dubbed voice of a boy witnessing the birth, saying *I've been to Paris but this is more beautiful. To me, it is more beautiful than Paris.*

Feeling a gust of warm air and a sudden tingling on their skin, the girls looked up, saw the men and heard the first orders. *The sea to be off limits soon. All boats to be safely tucked away.* They quickly rearranged themselves for a better viewing and made their choices. The oldest girl, who was nineteen and had high-arched brows and thin lips, predictably chose the leader of the pack, the man behind the megaphone. *People to move to the cyclone shelter. Everybody has a phone but nobody wants to watch the news.* The strokes in his bumper voice convinced her that he could easily lift her in his arms. She followed the contours of his persimmon uniform and imagined him bending just for her, just the two of them on the beach, making patterns in the sand. Heart within an unclasped heart: Kwality Wall's art.

The girl sitting next to her, who had a set of silver safety pins dangling down her neck, stared at the lone policeman behind the disaster management team. Young and thin with a head of curly hair, holding his lathi, he was leaning against a dusty motorbike. A khaki was never a pleasant sight in the neighbourhood, so her friends tried dissuading her with hushed signals, but the drab uniform reminded her so much of the curtains at the photo booth she liked, where she regularly lifted and dropped her chin on command but not very subtly, thus inviting a long, correcting hand. She had copied and shared videos with the photographer, who was also the source of the lambing clip. How similar the two men looked—the same boredom in the eyes and a strong noise pointing to the mouth—but their mouths were as opposite. The photographer's smile was dazzling white, offered up into the air like a fluttering napkin, a flag she could keep her eyes on when the day got fuzzy and also summon in her glutinous dreams. The khaki's was dark and slick, like a snowman's. It pulled her towards obsidian and promised no redemption. The man saw her and winked. A sharp urge rose to mince some meat; she felt her tongue flash into nothingness.

# 25

FAMILIAR WITH THE DRILL FOR the shelter, Luni began to pack. Clothes, phone, phone charger, work kit, a sheet, a shawl, keys, some jewellery, medicines and a steel box—all stuffed in a shoulder bag. Within the steel box were important documents secured in plastic bags, pieces of fabric, a knot holding Himmo's baby teeth and a smaller box filled with pouches of hair.

She carefully put Himmo's uniform and the handkerchief set in the embroidery hoop into her daughter's school bag. Added to the front pocket a couple of books, a packet of bread, their toothbrushes and paste. Once the bags were done and Himmo had tried hers on to see if she could carry it, Luni shifted them to the door and moved swiftly around the room. She placed items in steel containers and stowed them high on shelves and slabs. Then right before leaving, she folded a tiny pouch of money and tucked it in her bra under the right breast.

By the time they began walking to the bus that would take them to the shelter, the sky was a grim tear of grey gauze. Himmo wore her headband and a flimsy plastic poncho over her top and pants. Earlier, when Luni had pulled out a dress, Himmo had to remind her of the difficulties of hiking it up to squat in the common toilet while still running the risk of a damp and smelly hem. The goal, as always, was to stay dry and proper as long as possible.

On the way, Luni spotted her friend, the woman who had walked into the parlour and demanded all its power, and called out to her. She was hunched over a bucket, framed by a large hole in a wall, and upon hearing them, stood up straight. She draped her dupatta over her head and tucked the edge tight behind her ears before waving to them.

Come, come, I'm almost done, she called back.

Himmo ran to a smaller hole in the wall and thrust her arm inside.

Ticket please, she sang out.

The woman tugged at the other end with her cold, rough hands.

Sorry, full house, but do you want to help?

Himmo nodded and passed through the bigger hole to the other side.

Now wring it hard, the woman said. But make sure you wring it towards you.

Luni stepped forward to help her daughter. Water dripping, dribbling. The woman spread a petticoat on a cord strung between two stumps that had once been another wall and a toilet partition. On the floor nearby lay a pile of fishing nets.

This needs a lining, Luni said as she pegged a dress in place. I'll add it.

The woman nodded. She pulled out a pair of jeans and a white long-sleeved shirt. Her movements seemed slow and deliberate in contrast to the people scurrying past to get to the bus.

How are things at the sister-in-law's? Luni asked.

Crowded, she said plainly. We will soon have to find someplace else to go.

Won't they give you a place?

For now, it's a lot in a church somewhere.

That's no place.

The woman shrugged.

You have the papers for it?

The air made a bad bounce. Then the woman turned and snapped at Luni. Not everyone is as lucky as you.

Her voice was harsh, as if it had pierced through the shell and flesh outwards. Luni bore her friend's barb and held her head low. *Jabilli*, she mumbled to herself. The moon. A gumball to keep steady once the difference had been claimed that made the stars two-faced. Some are called to the sea and some are sent to it, and the strength of the sent could not have a better outcome. The woman's family had stayed long in the neighbourhood and owned a boat, whereas Luni's was a younger home and that too acquired on a loan.

Did I tell you about the gardeners? the woman said in a calmer voice as she emptied the bucket. One time, I saw four of them take shelter under a tree during heavy rain. Standing north, south, east and west. When lightning struck the trunk, they all fell—slowly, like a flower opening.

On the other side of the hole, each mind unfurled a different bud—lotus, rose, early lily. The woman moved closer to Himmo and crouched, opened her mouth and offered her tongue. The girl hesitated, then leaned forward and observed the red islands and spume. She touched the tender melting point under the tongue and wondered, why this scenario? She could have made the scorched trunk bloom—not the boughs or the branches, but the trunk itself. Or painted the hollow squishy gold. Himmo found an eyelash stuck on one side. She saw it for what it was, but in that alien place, that other world of tongue, what could it have been tethered to? A fallen latitude? Beyond the reaches of the young mind: the mighty Kanchenjunga's broken tide or a ripped mandorla. Maybe a sweet fermata that had strived to measure the will of the people. She dragged it out with her fingernail and held it to the sky.

Quick, make a wish, the woman said.

Himmo closed her eyes but before she could concentrate, she felt a tug on her poncho.

Wait, the woman said, looking back at the sea. Wait till I'm gone. Will you tell me the wish when I see you next?

Himmo shook her head.

The woman laughed, stood up, kissed the girl on the forehead and picked up the pail. She nodded at Luni, then walked away.

Later that night, when the sea roughened, no colour was precisely visible on the clothesline. Only dim shapes. Except for the prophet, who danced with his white arms swinging wildly in the wind, glazed for the touch of iris.

# 26

*TO THE DOG AT THE feet of the blue boy:*

*The womb ruptured in an animal body. The foetus flung across the bones and lodged under the skin near the armpit. How long can it survive in its new home?*

*Your master's blueness speaks:* Oh you make it so rare. *A wound should know what to grow into. Draw water from the womb. Then give nones the water.*

# 27

THE SCIENCE CENTRE WAS BARE and prepared. Partitions, furniture and equipment had been removed, and notices in different languages were stuck on the walls, each carrying a common message in bold print:

> *Please do not bring your gas cylinders to the cyclone shelter.*

A young palliative care doctor, tasked with operating one of the rooms as a sickbay, walked around counting the old and visibly pregnant, and observing the belongings of people as they arrived in the afternoon. Over the years, she had maintained a list of items that fascinated her: a pair of tongs, a jump rope, a quarter of a gold medal won in 100-metre hurdles that had been split among brothers, a pack of Phantom cigarettes, an empty surgical glove box. A puppet to be mastered from below but only with the right hand, a barely chewed bar of hotel soap. She recognized the need for these objects—things that could help start a life and things that could help endure it. No matter how meagre or useless they may seem, like the cluster of pens pulled clear out of squids and kept under the pillow on the terminal bed; or the little palette of green eyeshadow she carried in her own coat pocket, to wear sometime or perhaps never wear.

Once a newlywed had walked into the shelter, thick vermilion smeared in her parting and arms wrapped around her bundled trousseau. There were those who had looked at her heavily sequinned sari and scowled—for where did she think she was going and to do what? Looking like a river fish and nothing else. So what if that clean-shaven husband of hers had promised her a honeymoon somewhere? So what if he could read a bit of English? She was a colour up but was this the time to show off? Oh how they wanted to hold her down and scrape off all that shimmer, for her own sake. She needed to be sober at such a time. But the doctor had been more bothered by the loose locks swaying behind her that spoke of a dreadful sea of threads. Black threads, matted threads—threads of girls and women who had drowned in droves one day after Christmas. Unlike the men who had known to run away from the waves, up trees and hills; keep their heads above water; thrash, thrash through the wreck, rip themselves off themselves and finally rise, mud-caked, raked and bare as Adam, ready to water the first weed that wanted to gasp out and live.

The women, meanwhile, trapped by duty to their loved ones and the very thing they thought gave them currency—a forehead curl to mark the spouse's fortune or a well-padded scalp that woke a cousin's envy—got tangled in glass, metal, branches and bushes; did not seek higher ground if the waves had stripped them naked; and were found gashed, wrapped, strangled, without fingers and toes, clinging to their old and young.

Out of the general flotsam that had swirled and drifted ever since and found its missing pieces on faraway shores, came a girl in a festive sweater and a woman dropping parcels into the sea. To the girl, the doctor had said that the MERRY across her chest really brought out her eyes and to the woman, she asked what was wrapped so lovingly.

Crispy skin! the woman cried. It came out crispier than before. It came out like a sock. I fried it.

The bride at the cyclone shelter had walked through the stubborn fog of dismay and disapproval, and spent the entire storm tying holy strings around a crate of bottled water. There were those who had looked on and said nothing.

# 28

GUL SOUNDED HOARSE ON THE phone as she spoke to a customer service agent.

It's been fifteen days.

I'm so sorry, ma'am. Let me check, please. Ma'am, I'm looking at your order, and it says it was received by the watchman.

I don't have a watchman. Check again.

Kindly hold.

Gul shook her head. She should have known from the packaging and ignored the four stars. After all, there were only so many ways to announce that a product was unique in quality, and genuine and original.

Ma'am, are you there?

Yes, yes.

Thank you for waiting. Ma'am, we have a set of initials on record.

But I—What initials! Ridiculous!

Ma'am, it says AR—

Gul cut the call.

Outside, at a fairly good distance, the sea had been cordoned off with a wall of bulky sandbags along the shore and rescue teams were stationed in place. Inside, Arth was darting around the house: bolting windows before the wind picked up speed, charging devices and batteries, and scanning the fridge for perishables in case of a long power cut. Gul sank further into the armchair by her bed, her eyes wan, teeth unbrushed. On the wall in front of her hung a bigger barasingha. God in a long ruffle skirt, who takes only two blind children when the stones fall. Who batters the nunneries but spares the swaying brothels; who makes the tenor throw open his window and belt out his grandest note.

A spider shone in its delicate web spun between the antlers, which clashed with the television box below. A soggy reporter was bending to interview a head floating in floodwater. *What do you want from the government?* A loud, anguished cry for help, and then the camera panned back to the reporter. The head, unaware of the generosity of the lens, quietly rose and walked out of the frame.

Gul was tuned out of the performance. In any case, the whole thing was askew. When the operators of a radio station had agitated for their rights, the channels called it an 'AIR STRIKE'. Not to forget the endless interviews between news segments with actors playing soldiers in films. Their sad, old template of honour and slaughter. Gul only put those channels on when she needed the volume or wanted to despise it. She believed it was a matter of time before they'd take it all the way and bring out the soldier playing a soldier in films. Him taking aim so gracefully with his replica rifle, straight at you, straight at the audience; crouching in the trench, not careless with his height; scaling a cliffside to the sounds of heavy guitar; collecting knees; and that bright, parabolic arc of his indomitable, squeeze bottle grenade—now that could be a thing worth watching.

She sat with a brush full of hair in her lap, feeling hideous, betrayed, like a frayed integer. Spent, like a scent stick. It was a calving so abrupt that it far surpassed the horrors of menopause, which itself had been brutal—shamelessly ruining clothes, car seats and office chairs, inviting the world's concerns and awkward comments. She felt a quiver in her left thigh and wanted it to stop. What could have caused this utter defeat? It was not as if she hadn't anticipated the glitter to split or not sensed the acoustics changing. Over the years, her reverberations had reduced remarkably. She now dreamt less of the tumult of lava and more of the surge of sweet volcano brine. Yet for some reason, this loss made her feel desperate, as though next, all the faults would rupture together. Perhaps it was the way she had glared at her younger colleague the other day that had done it. The one who had enthusiastically swayed from theorizing on geological unconformities—gaps of missing time in the rock record—to bombing the vents of Mauna Loa and mopping the flow. Watching the bombing through a telescope.

Your bomb is weak, Gul had said quite bluntly.

Now in her room, she regretted it. She had to let the woman gain her insights. Let her prod the line and discover how a desire line can be a rescue line, unlike a bloodline or a wasteline. She recalled how, at her own engagement party, the colleague had used geodes to keep the rings instead of the usual velvet boxes. Nestled on a gold tray among ripples of soft pale silk and loose pearls—glimmering quartz for herself and amethyst for her groom. Enchanted by the display, when Gul had expressed a desire to do something similar for her daughter's wedding, the woman had gifted her the rocks under the daunting eyes of relatives, a gesture that had touched her deeply. The two sets of halves were now placed in front of her oils on the dresser, and sometimes, on deep, dew-whisked nights, Gul liked to take them out to the garden and set them at the base of a beautiful bonsai, thinking of the man who sat whipping foam and gathering bling for all of life's prosthetics. She was his preparation. He'd stroke his limb as if it wasn't there, then sit folded on shoes pointed backwards, so that the knees sported tranquil smiles. He instructed her with the aid of the miniature tree, whose virtuous trunk curved out of a rugged pot, giving it the impression of growing off a wind-beaten cliff. *The subtle branches must not criss-cross,* he reminded her. *There is dignity in the pot.*

Gul sat up a bit and put the brush on the chair to her right. The door to her room was closed. She lifted her legs and placed her feet slightly apart on the side of the bed. Bunched the hem of her nightgown close to her stomach and moved her hand between her thighs. The quiver turned into small, spilling waves. She slid the last cloth aside to wander in the tufts, then pinched a bunch between her thumb and forefinger. She twisted its top, and with the other hand pressing down on the skin, pulled with a jerk. Wild black bouquet with bulbs glistening white—a split end and a single white strand. Fully white. She threw it all on the floor and kept plucking. Beneath her, starlings assembled in thick black traffic: a perfect redaction—an ordinary season, a themeless sky.

# 29

SOMEONE HAD BROUGHT A PARROT to the shelter. The creature, lonely for a touch screen, had been dyed pope pink so as to appeal as an exotic species; but its unmistakable green screech gave it away. *Two fat ladies 88*. It delighted the children gathered around the cage but bothered the owner, for it was calling out numbers in a hurry and risking a riot. One time, during a tambola night held to raise funds for charity, it had gone so fast that a brawl had broken out over corners.

The shelter was packed, and earlier, there had been commotion as people claimed their spaces and spread out their belongings. Adults stood in line to receive food parcels. The disaster response men carried in the priestess from the neighbourhood after she'd refused to part with her indie, who she claimed had been impregnated by the wind. The dog would scratch down the walls of her house, she'd pleaded. Her swollen nipples were already dripping milk.

Now finding herself next to the parrot, the old woman did her best to match its shrill voice.

Let me be ripped to pieces! I have lived long enough. Let the sea take me!

Then suddenly, she stopped. The doctor strode in to investigate what had interrupted her and found the old woman staring at a wide wall of the main hall, where, behind the pasted notices, stretched out an enormous whale shark. Its gaping mouth dominating the body.

They knew what it was and they killed it, the doctor muttered and then instantly felt the shock. Her work was preparing for and dignifying the end, not courting rage. Most definitely, she thought, the reaction was the consequence of the bell between the wards. She had advocated fiercely for its place to be changed. For the sake of the living incurable, who could not participate in someone else's relief from suffering; who had rung it before and returned to the pain; and now asked only to be able to sleep through the night, longed only for the toll of silence. One of whom had said to her, *you're my single window, doc.* For whom she had lifted a short purple pencil high above her head during each visit, steering his fear, like a tour guide. Past the loud hawkers of agony and death pressing in from all sides, past the people and buses both ahead and behind, she took him to his sweet self at the end, selling only love. *Mohabbat ka thanda meetha sharbat.* A cool, sweet potion of love.

After he passed, she kept the pencil in the hope of guiding others along. The blunt nib had chipped at the top, making a mouth, which, when it touched the page, produced two lines. It was the thought of this second, fainter line around letters, which she called the sarcophagus, that made the doctor gather herself and resee the creature on the wall as one not mourned like the whale. Perhaps because not much is known about when or where the female gives birth. Its belly is no popular hell; the thousand and more docile teeth—no jawbone for a fence. No struck skull hanging from the ceiling, dripping oil; no ambergris to distract from the body's sounds, which, under the influence, carry. No eternal fixation that bestows it leviathan names such as War and Peace or Glory, Hope, Faith and Grace; its fall in the deep no copious glory to be thus described—*whale debrided, refugia, oasis, whale colonized.* Whales are the sounds of the universe. Chronic witnesses. The doctor sighed. Plus, a whale named Hyphen could only mean that the world ever shreds halfway, and the whale shark's opacity induces but little remorse.

The men, women and children in the room turned towards the mural, following the bony priestess, who leaned forward. As they watched, the dots began to move. The room darkened and the doctor found it hard to pull air. The people gaped, their eyes big and fingers pointing. The being was clutching them. It had plucked itself out of the wall and was slowly drifting overhead, like a big balloon. A slant of light through every pore. The old woman began to chant in a breathy voice:

> *tuki tuki papa tuki tuki tuki papa tuki papa tuki tuki papa*

The others joined in.

> *tuki papa tuki papa papa tuki tuki*

The doctor couldn't make sense of what they were saying. When the whale shark passed close to her, she tried to read its skin for a message. Something about ice. *Put it on ice?*

After a while, once the trance had lifted, the old woman rubbed her eyes and poked her ears as if to get the water out. Then she turned to the children behind her.

Do you want to hear a story? she said.

The children nodded. She broke into a tale in hurried sentences about a ruler who dreamt only of his great old mother rushing down a playground slide, and who himself had been ageless until one day he suddenly dropped dead while touring the country. His most trusted men did not know what to do but soon discovered orders stitched inside his sleeve to conceal the truth in case of an untimely demise till the convoy reached the capital, so there could be a proper funeral with a feast. His men put him to rest in his carriage and got a bunch of fishermen to travel along with carts of rotting dolphins, hoping that the smell would ward off any suspicion. They tucked one dolphin in his bed, its beak clasped shut with a gold ring. The ruler's face was sweet again, softened, like a sugar cube held on the tongue long enough.

The mouth dies last, the old woman said, dropping her voice. The mouth does not die at all!

No sooner had she revealed this than an ancient wind began to wail around the shelter. The children huddled together, feeling guilty. The wail got sharper. A man in the corner began to make from what was vacant in his hands, propped against his chin—the whorl from the bandstand, the frill for the ban, the thing that was teething. He pulled at the crane nipple, pushed a bit—the top drawer, the smock drawer pulled again: the sea.

The priestess snapped shut. She stayed like that for hours till a little hand peeped through and mistook the snatch for life.

# 30

THE POWER WENT OUT AND Arth situated herself outside her mother's bedroom door. It was closed from inside from inside and she could sense it was because of the hair. The walls of the house had started developing stains, and old towels were tucked in crevices under doors and windows. She sat on the floor with a portable lamp, a pack of biscuits and a glass of water. Arth had checked if her neighbour too was in the dark and, finding it to be the case, felt comforted by it. Now she sat, trying to relax, but her mind returned a nugget from a long time ago: *Hush, hush, gorah daktar is coming. The horse doctor.* Arth had sprayed stuff out of her nose and mouth the first time she'd read the lines in an international paper, but this time she was content with a smile. Of course it was the horse doctor. He had come at this hour to ride the chicken, the pig and the horn; to give them medicine for worms in horses; to treat their inward-bound laughter that wove the stallion's mane and the limbs of the panopticon. And if the fowl resisted too much, he had with him his lofty invention, a sequence he so proudly called 'the eclipse'—of something to anaesthetize, something to paralyse and the acid that stops the heart. Though a severe dose of the first component could kill in itself, the combination aspired to the divine balance of grace and punishment, but carried out humanely, the evidence of which was the middle drug. It was added solely for the sake of the witness. To seize in case the grace proved inadequate, so that the viewer does not see the victim flinching, the rebel thrashing, the enemy gasping for breath—this choice, made sometimes in the name of the dignity of the condemned, was what ensured the totality of the event and allowed one to look directly at it.

Let it stay a storm, Arth thought. Not all are as wild as him. The dentist is gentle; he knows the third world lies in the teeth. His hands will touch the sharp tips for pleasure, then scrape off all virtue to give you speech. He'll find and save those specks of lazuli.

Arth dunked a biscuit into her glass and drenched the raised G, then ate it. She knocked on the door.

Open up, Ma. Don't do this.

She wanted no part of the drama, but her mother couldn't just be left alone. Not when Gul's acceptance of the geological continuum, which she liked to frame in the kitchen as 'most people are afraid of flipping stuff but not me', had failed at the limits of her own body. The otherwise decisive body that had coolly escorted the eras and exercised an even temperament during difficulties, so much so that when Gul was asked how soon after her father's death had she proceeded to stand in front of the mirror and exfoliate, brought out the gold-flecked day and night creams, she had answered with ease: four wayward calls. Even if days had grown like stalactites inside her, Gul must have welcomed it. But here she was, like limestone giving in on itself, unable to rationalize the threat. Perhaps because the idea of elsewhere is ultimately inescapable, Arth thought. It is life's preservative, and being is a beautiful dwindling bird that survives on this tree. Try to cut down the tree after calling it invasive, risk losing the bird. Adorn it to the point of fetishizing it, burden it with all your hopes, and life becomes more and more remote to itself, unfree from expectation and therefore ruthless, even mythical in nature.

In Gul's case, the tree was harder to diminish, not only because her denial fortified it, but also a facet of it was explicit, rooted in her very name and present in pivotal moments of her life—her father's persistent cough, her mother's fatal delivery. Could the most profound of all elsewheres then be lost childhood, the loss becoming more palpable with both parents' demise? And more so if the child herself was gone, as seen in the case of the linen ball buried along with an Egyptian girl thousands of years ago that shows up in the hands of a young refugee in modern times. *For play in the afterlife.* So it must be, it must be, at most a trace fossil, not even a feather, for one should be able to bear a loss no less, or else.

Arth waited a while before calling out again.

Open the door, Ma.

There was no answer.

No one cares about your hair.

But she did care, and she dreaded clearing the bin. If only a little dried bread could soften the outline in real life and make Gul's limits more breathable. If only she could bring back the glory days of Gul's frothy palimpsest, the circuits of shimmer, the slow cinch of unbraiding. Dark rivers tumbling down her back as she guided an insect out the window while announcing in a singsong voice:

*Ting ting tingg. Yaatrigan kripaya dhyaan dein. May I have your attention please ...* Blaring past the station of basket weavers pulling stitches out of sixes. Carriages full of families spilling out in corridors that smell of fried food and days-old flatulence; children gathered at the sink for a very public ceremony of brushing and spitting; and a boy, partly hanging off the top berth, alive to the infinite track, tingling due to his proximity to the chain. What passes by—goats in the purple grass and the runaway mustard, homes never finished, the inaudible lowing; and what is underneath—a rain-filled tunnel for the silent march from the village to the grave. The dead and the living sitting on the tracks ahead, some squatting. Wanting something. Demanding something. Daring you to look away.

Then there is the darkness that blots out the page, save for the occasional flash of light that brings back a word or two. In this absence or in the pitch-black night, while a cable softly taps against the window, there is love and destitution in the corners, by the rat traps and open doors. And sometimes, an evil so abject as to be struck by its own despair may catch up and break in stark naked, only to bathe one fully clothed. Yes, something will perish out of shock alone, but the word can save us. A whole coach crushes bottles, stomping on the bear's head. Green on the other end. A painter's green of two summers. A passing train's evergreen. A little bit of red can make any green out of the tube more natural. Then another station with its set of basket makers pulling out stitches, but no, not the eight of eighteen. Catch the flying name. Knuckles on the palms eighteen. All it would take is a coin in the joint of the tracks. Arth banged on the door.

Open up!

The latch clicked. Arth hurried into the dim room and caught Gul's shape sinking into a vortex of sheets. She made her way towards her mother's face, then suddenly recoiled. The feeling of breaching some necessary boundary that protected the levels in their relationship—that kept Gul away from her daughter's pity—had gripped Arth once before, when she'd spied her mother dancing in circles in her bedroom like she'd lost her mind, her face loose. Gul never came to know but Arth had been unable to look at her straight for days after, and when required, only stared at her wrists. And this was much worse.

Her mother looked haggard, chewed up, her hand clutching a braided segment adorned with drying chilli peppers. She had wet the bed.

One look at her sapless eyes and Arth sprang into action. She placed the lamp on the dressing table and helped her mother up. Gathered towels from the bathroom and admonished the sheets—a flock of strays took flight. She sprinkled baking soda and vinegar on the mattress stain while watching her mother who stood by the armchair with her head down and eyes closed. She opened the cupboard and pulled out fresh clothes. Then she walked over and stripped off Gul's sogginess, talking all the while about a future visit to the library of volcanic dust to swoon over samples from all over the globe, some more than two hundred years old. It was maintained by a woman in her nineties who had survived tuberculosis and two shipwrecks, and had even dived at one of the sites to bring back two cups and a bowl. It was a trip her mother had always wanted to make.

Arth wiped her, thinking there was something so beautiful about this fate. That the river floods the poet who spends his whole life singing her; who goes back into her looking for bricks. She bent down and stretched the holes of Gul's underwear for her to put her feet through, then hooped a dry nightgown over her head and threw the brush kept on the armchair into the bin. Gul sighed as she sat in the chair. She kept her eyes shut. Arth used another brush to comb her mother's hair, which fell a few inches below the shoulder. She groomed her like a chimp would groom its dead infant, even after the head had rolled off on the eighteenth day.

Finally, once Arth had dragged a spare mattress to the foot of the bed, brought over pillows from her room, tucked the edges of a fresh sheet under the mattress and piled all the soiled linen in the bathroom under the sink, she helped her mother down gently and set the braided segment beside her.

It's nothing, Ma, she said softly. Nothing at all.

Nothing. Dial it down, down. Down: sleepless nights in the scent of steamed nappies. Down: samples collected in empty medicine bottles with impossibly narrow mouths. It was nothing at all. Gul could have written her way out with it, Arth thought. She would examine with the iron the next day.

When she tried to move away after a while, Gul reached out and held her hand. A current bolted them together and brought them back to the steep steps of the blue tomb, where Arth had first registered her mother's strange, cold grasp on their way down. She was almost sixteen by then. Gul wasn't big on holding hands. The ruler whose tomb it was had died falling down those same steps.

Now Arth felt the same need seeking her, so she swung a leg over her mother and hovered above. Careful not to put her weight down, she gazed at the slight curves under her.

Gul's mouth and her torn lips—dark rose and raw where she had punctured herself. Arth touched the tip of her mother's tongue with her finger—the muscle that had taught her to lick rocks. The salty halite, the sharp bitter note of sylvite, the fossil that sticks to the base. The trophy bone, the smooth centre—Gul on her knees for that change of heart. With her head leaned against the earth, wishing for the luck of the scientist who had discovered five dinosaur eggs just by bending down to tie his shoelaces. Arth smiled as she remembered her mother's lips moving quietly by roadcuts and in stony parks. Her hand lightly dented Gul's throat as it moved down to the silver asterisks around her neck—her grandmother's charms that they had to take off her body to pass on. She lifted it on her fingers. Hedgehogs, Gul called them. Beneath the chain were dots across her collarbone, which, as a child, Arth had connected using a kohl stick: a ladle and a seahorse. But there was another cluster somewhere that she had not joined. Gul had mentioned it a few times without ever telling what constellation it made or on which part. Arth wanted to find it. She pulled back, then peeled her mother's nightgown till the base of her breasts, so that the trails on the stomach were available to her. Most of them meandered murky; others flowed silver. Arth leaned closer and heard them hissing: *terra firma terra incognita terra pericolosa.* Coming to places where reeds would bloom through lace, where the salt floes made a wife. Tracing the subsidence and striations, the caverns and craters, the wide floodplain. Arth's hands on her mother, building a reef.

She moved gently at first, then fondled with urgency. An illegible coercion taking over. The pitch of Gul's bladder, the pour of her lips repugnant no more. From the deepest crevices, Arth caught a whiff of something sour and it made her salivate. Her rhythms in such a frenzy that she forgot about the dots. Tried scooping up the navel, but it got away—that roaming thing, winking socket. That roaming thing; winking socket. When she finally succeeded, she found a sea anemone or a sun slithering out. Leftover ruby. Jasper den. Bodies of sphene and chalcocite. And just when the edge of a new thing was about to make itself known, Arth winced. She had felt Gul swelling.

A daughter all her life bathes in the rumour of that sea which remains but a single piece of silver confetti. But here it was, a prism webbed and moist, an inkling of orogeny. Looking away and up at the dresser, Arth slid off to the side. The geodes sat twinkling in front of the dark oils. She got up and quietly left the room.

After the door closed, Gul regarded the chattering of loosely fitted glass. She raised a key and dipped it in. A canned spiral tickled into motion—waves tossing high, then higher, cliffs jutting and, oh, the Brahmaputra sliding back. The suck of the mud for each limb. There were two of them and they were leaning on her on either side. She needed them just like that, just talking. *There there there.* Their voices like a blaze working its way up the natural history museum. *A hole in the bucket dear Liza dear Liza there's a hole in the bucket* ... The flamingo's pink legs like leashes burning—Gul heard the door open and hurried to take the finger out.

Arth walked in, turned off the lamp and lay down next to her mother. She pretended to have glimpsed nothing. But since all silence in a storm is storm-born, the room grew bold and then Arth moaned, pulled Gul in by the hips and sealed her mouth onto her mother's.

The breath made invincible by homemade white butter. Gul welcomed it like a conch.

# 31

THERE WAS A BRITTLE STAR with a pulse unfurling between her legs. Her hands: a codex on thread. Luni kept shifting her weight from one foot to the other as she catered to the women who sat in line, waiting to get their eyebrows done. What else was there to do in the face of all that fury? Luni had deduced the answer over time: Make it up. Unspool the thread when there's enough to go around. Between women, she looked up and saw the Himalayas drenched red.

Working in a corner of the hall, she got what help she could from the two thin, generator-run tube lights up above, and the line ran along the side of the room. The night looked over her shoulder as if to learn the different features so it could paint itself a set. She wondered what else it did—take the masks out and arrange and arrange the screams till the storm lost all specificity?

Her daughter sat nearby in the maze of men and children spelling up and down in sleep. Himmo and the boy she'd bit were next to a big jar of dried jackfruit, making calculations and devising strategies to tackle the mass of flip-flops that would be thrown up by the sea. All to avail that nice thing that waited at the junk shop.

Could she pay in Halls, Himmo wondered, just in case no pair was good enough? In a dream, she had searched her pockets and pulled out a fuschia queen. Or could she offer two bright pairs to the dealer or should she clean and put back a few decent rubbers as decoys on the beach? It was clear to her what the prize was and she could feel it rolling inside: a die made of pearl. She'd play it and make the dolls speak. She'd throw it again and play herself.

Luni made the women sit on a chair one by one, their faces tilted up as she leaned over from behind, their hands stretching the skin tight around their powdered brows. The person leaving the chair shone a phone torch on the forehead of the next in line, adding to the tube lights. Luni worked on taming the edges, a cotton thread twisted tight between her teeth and fingers. Correcting, cleaning, reconsidering to keep the frame thick or thin, straight, long or short, high-arched or sympathetic, depending upon the face's needs. There were women who hummed as they waited, while others discussed after-storm fixups and the mangrove planting drive to be held in the coming months. A paid opportunity to pose for brochure photos. Sun-spangled angels with their legs sinking in the mud; women brandishing wand-like saplings as though those were instruments of their martyrdom. An annual gratitude feast would also be organized for the guest of honour, the chief minister, and, among other things, the women would serve up his favourites—pickled mackerel, prawn biryani and coconut buns. Once, in a non-election year, they'd fed his spectacled son instead and watched as the aides made a fuss in front of the cameras about gifting five litres of cooking oil and a few bags of rice for the entire neighbourhood.

Someone whispering about avoiding the event and instead joining a protest against the demolitions was gently but quickly shut down. Not because the people inside the shelter were resigned to their fate, or exhausted, ignorant and afraid, but because they deemed the discussion of the matter unsuitable for the situation they were in. Having been moved not so much inland as upwards, like the farmer but less so—still in suspension, the fisherman was, despite what it seemed, less spirit than flesh, more flesh *vague* with spirit, and the only right thing to do then was to attend to the palpable forces of nature and time, the primordial tussle between land and water. To not pay heed to what humans did in their greed to aggravate, appropriate and make into a struggle between hostile land and irascible water; but to that pure chaos of birth and death, being wrenched out of the water and returned to it, for any separation between the two powers was purely fictional—the land was, is and will again be water; water is land at its deepest. The fisherman knew that to survive on such a constructed seam, at the changing point where both are claimed—ostracism and indifference, visibility and invisibility—was to live, love and fully exist as the mockery of it. In the dark hours, when he was both sky and earth, land and water, the farmer liberated above and the soldier down below, the fisherman cared first not to disrupt by distraction or schemes or even a too-rapid heartbeat, the main whistling, circling power. A woman secretly wishing to slip a hair or two into the spectacled son's soup would be, for now, the extent of their revolt.

Luni's mind ambled to the person she knew loved prawn biryani the most, and how strange it had been to find him beautiful. To caress the top of his bald head, feel the stunted horn. There had been whispers about a girl he'd loved only for a night, who then went and jumped into the sea. Luni believed it and craved the thing that was unleashed. To be on the cusp of it had already bent her nail clippings into perfect crescents and led her to discover the delicacy of her own gaze. Such power and release upon his smallest parts. Aching, untouched, until out of ache. When finally reached, then re-ached. What scent could she pipe into this dome.

She smiled. She could have never imagined getting tangled up this way, least of all with him. He had been consigned to that sympathetic place where her sweet client Annie lay in the grass with her scalp showing through her thin platinum hair, until the night they had their first meal together. She'd served him the simple ecstasy of hot boiled potatoes with freshly ground chillies and a glass of chilled sugarcane juice, and he'd said that was all the summer there was to remember. Moving closer in the kitchen as she proceeded to wash the dishes, he'd lifted the hem of her long skirt and quietly wiped his hands.

Soon after, she'd stitched white lace into a glove to keep it a hand. To feel that lace break warm on her thighs, melt smooth and smear like vanilla frosting. But there was one thing that had puzzled her throughout their time together: what kind of a man ran out of spit?

Her stomach creaked in agony. Her pad itched. She had the paper for it—some ripped unread piece about stress management workshops for lottery winners. There was a creeping smell of damp metal and Luni felt grateful for it, even though she had started bleeding much earlier than most women she knew and her flow could get quite heavy, for it told her that her womb was blocked by no baby and she was safe. The blood surprised her with the shapes it made, but that had not always been the case. Back when she was with her husband, it had been too preoccupied with the task of keeping him off, which left it dull and unanimated. The moment she'd say that she had spoiled her legs and sometimes show proof of it, he dared not touch her. She'd keep the stained underwear to wear an extra day, and once, she'd slit a chicken to make the stains. But all that was long past, as was the memory of the wedding-night streak made so thin by promises. What mattered now was that the dead blood bloomed poppies; birthed stars; tinged wings, obelisk and mountaintops; and rolled thick between the banks of a woman who could love freely.

Luni wanted to yank the dangling arm and set it on its way, but the toilet reeked of faeces. The last user, who had proudly spent the bulk of her savings to build a 'world-class' pay-and-use toilet in her native village (for which she had even organized a proper inauguration with ribbon-cutting and drums), had come raging out the door and that was enough filth to do a reading, like how some fancy people read tea leaves. Enough to see which bones dissolved and which did not. Luni wanted to get far from all of it, so she looked up, but the night conceded nothing. The Himalayas were gone, but somewhere inside, she could still feel them resisting. Perhaps the nastiness had let them down. She changed foot again, this time to press back into pleasure, a little tap for its membership, but by then the bed had transformed: into the yellow, jagged claw of an excavator.

# 32

IN THE FOLLOWING DAYS, NEWS arrived that a barge of an oil and gas corporation, having gone adrift after the storm snapped its anchors, had sunk into the Arabian Sea, claiming at least forty-five Brave Nature Victims. The navy was still conducting search-and-rescue operations.

Over 9,000 villages lost power in Gujarat. Lions could be heard roaring outside houses fringing Gir.

A popular zoo, which was to soon host a first birthday party for its white tiger cub—with meat treats and bones for the carnivores; corn for the birds; rice ladoos, fruits and banana tree stalks for the elephants; sugar-free jellies for the chimps; sugar-laden cakes and cutouts for the humans—had suffered great damages. Enclosures were in shambles, trees uprooted, nets ripped apart and several animals missing: three pythons; one leopard; hundreds of birds, bees, butterflies and other insects; and a penguin. Two black bucks, a barking deer and four antelopes had died from the sound of the storm.

Nearly three hundred newborns were registered in Gujarat's hospitals, health centres and shelters during the storm. Eighty were named Sangai.

At the hotel on the beach in the town where Gul, Arth, Luni and Himmo lived, constant power supply had been maintained for the aquarium to ensure the health of the fish, and no injuries were sustained by the gymnasium fitted with high-quality, double-glazed glass. Collection bins were now set up next to the guest book in a corner of the lobby where anyone could come and donate, and so far the staff had gathered food and milk packets, sheets, blankets, hygiene kits, a used stiletto and a wig.

# 33

*TO THE WOMAN REPLACED BY a bloodstain:*

*Nerik gave birth to something resembling the eggs of a sea turtle, and Flora gave birth to something like intestines. One with spikes everywhere, except in the part where she broke off from her mother. Another born in a caul; the membrane dried and kept safe in a suitcase.*

*Sitting in the same room with a molar in your fist, you hear them say: How foolish to be expecting at this time! How careless! No puffiness to this flat host! Now where will the colony seat you?*

*They lift the old server from his wheelchair and bring him to the ballot box, his legs dangling in the air. You point: in that reasonable air.*

*You'll still have to dance for your portion.*

*I'll dance.*

*Check my polish*
*and my willing cast of breath.*

*Let me pass*
*with my phantom knocking*

*to where my dancing is not a slur.*

# 34

The day after the storm, Gul walked out the door without a braid. The transparency felt terrible. The lightness demanded simple courage.

Let it land, she told herself.

Her daughter had wrapped a scarf around her head to ease the pressure on her roots. Gul walked past wronged trees and roads and clothes draped on street signs till she reached the beach and found the wall punctured. A sandbag heart was weeping a waterfall. As soon as she put her palm below it, she knew: it was her father.

*Yes, let it land*, he repeated. *The wrist knows to rinse itself.*

Gul had often wondered if he should have gone like a seed instead, upright in a vessel, so that the reading of his return could be easier, for it had been anything but that. She'd found a streetlamp burning in daylight and thought it was him. She had pawed its compartment for any confirming sign. And, when a woman walked up a slope with a balloon shop rigged to a stroller, Gul again thought it was him in that hooded darkness she was speaking to so softly. She had crossed the road when something stopped her steps and she knew the stroller was empty. The balloon seller, smiling, had skipped the ladybirds, cartoons and footballs, and untied the only unsigned heart for her.

Gul had looked for her father in blank calls and seaweed patterns; in old men fluttering on the beach, mute and hectic, like a flag. Now finally, here he was, streaming into her cupped hand.

Baba, she said. Baba. She had heard him clearly, yet her approach was tentative, as though she'd found in the labyrinths of sacred texts and manuscripts a mention of a lost or coming earthquake:

*And when he had cried out again in a loud voice, he gave up his spirit. At that moment the curtain of the temple was torn in two from top to bottom. The earth shook, the rocks split and the tombs broke open.*

*Then she, in a yellow robe, with joined palms and her*

*head bowed, her eyes lowered, said, 'If in thought, I have never dwelt on any but him, may Goddess Earth receive me.' And she did.*

*Cities and villages have become mounds of stone, and men and women from those same places had come here in pale white dresses with their horses and mules and donkeys loaded with bread and food and wine in order to hold the hand of the poor.*

*That day, mankind will issue forth in scattered groups to be shown their deeds.*
*And whoso doeth good an atom's weight will see it then, and whoso doeth evil an atom's weight will see it then.*

Yellow robe. Pale white dresses. It struck her—the orange colour of the sandbag. During one of the Geology Mondays at the science centre, a boy with a bowl cut had raised his hand and sincerely asked a question: *Miss, what colour is an earthquake?*

Gul had dealt with peculiar answers before, such as the time when she'd put up a map of an estuary and asked the students what it was, and a kid said it resembled a man in a gas mask but never had she encountered such an odd question. Even the maths problem that had thrown off her father had only amused her:

> *A and B together contribute 100 rupees to the Prime Minister's Relief Fund to help earthquake victims. Write a linear equation to satisfy the above data and draw its graph [for 3 marks].*

Remembering how he'd read the exam paper over and over again, she thought about his way of teaching that stood against almost everything being practised in current classrooms—breaking a child's hand because she could not spell 'parrot' or beating a boy for asking why, in chemistry, there were so many exceptions to the rule. Gul took particular pride in following in her father's footsteps: keeping her views independent and her command as gentle as she could; responding to each and every query, even those that were just a few lines on the forehead or a scratching of the cheek, nothing sung or spoken. During a visit to the natural history museum in the months before the fire, Gul had tapped into her instincts and, reading what was written on her daughter's face, replied swiftly: Sometimes, what you see folding is the ankle.

So when the boy with the bowl cut asked her a question that left her flummoxed, Gul did the only thing she could think.

What do you mean, what colour it is? she asked. Do you know?

Which one? he replied, smudging a place in an atlas with his sticky caramel fingers.

Ah yes, which one. There are two types of wounds that the earth makes, she'd taught the students, one for vanity and one to nest in. We enter the latter through the other.

Orange, the boy said.

For days after, she had stared at shake maps posted on a citizen reporting website called 'Did You Feel It?'. Red, blue, green dots marking values formulated from a questionnaire:

*Were you asleep?*
*Not specified*
*I was not sleeping*
*Slept through it*
*Woke up*

*Did others nearby feel it?*
*Not specified*
*No others felt it*
*Some felt it, most did not*
*Most felt it*
*Everyone/almost everyone felt it*

*How would you best describe your reaction?*
*Not specified*
*No reaction/not felt*
*Very little reaction*
*Excitement*
*Somewhat frightened*
*Very frightened*
*Extremely frightened*

*How did you respond?*
*Not specified*
*Took no action*
*Moved to doorway*
*Dropped and covered*
*Ran outside*
*Other*
*Please describe:*

Cartographic pigments symbolic of human experience. Gul had wondered: If an earthquake is an expression of the earth felt by man, then could it not have colour? Take, for instance, happiness. A person rushes down eleven flights of stairs; others are paralysed by it. Sometimes, a girl is lifted out of the rubble of sadness like a trophy. And when the earth takes away both master and slave curled up in the end like lovers, surely there is colour to such pride.

The boy had known this, had had access to it, while she, whose body jerked and rippled every day, had not. Gul thought about the purpose of this different deformation. There'd been a certainty to his careless response. Who was nearer, somehow, and what had he lost for this. And if she tried, could her earthquakes have colour as well?

All paths led to the varves. Gul pulled up a series of light and dark remembrances and inspected their textures for streaks and pollen beds, but orange hovered over every record. Over the red of Republic Day, red bus, red rudder, bright red reek eked. The strawberry finch staked upon the signal, but he hadn't wanted them to remember him this way. No. See the close white dots along the lower lid and keep the bird pure, he'd said. Despite the first wayward call: *did he do it, did you do it, did he do it, did you do it*. Keep the songbird pure, like the snow falling as he wrote on the blackboard with both arms outstretched. The pure bill and then the cockroach on the drain cover of her shower. The green of her first apophyllite. Two grey flukes that made the story of birth; the indigo of illness. Still grey was the day when Arth ran away, but with a blue bias; pending blue was a cold hand kept upon a pining chest. Then a little fountain of yellow rising, with eyes closed, to finally prick the orange, which gushed into a flurry of golden dead bees and chunks of honey.

So Gul scooped some up with a crust. She went home and made a list:

orange
antiseptic
fire/escape
drizzle on white cake
must count before the final squeeze
pop rocks
pickling liquid
blood/orange
black box
scissors for tags and red meat
a door swinging—

Gul chose orange to colour the hinges.

# 35

EJECTED INTO SHIRRED LIGHT, PAST the mess of plumeria over the shrine, the residents of the neighbourhood stood on the beach in remade air. The priestess cooed and cradled fresh puppies, the indie close behind her.

Luni stood lost in a photograph the doctor had shown her at the shelter: a desert marked by snow. The white satin moult of an ochre grin. She had called it Sahara. Luni wondered if it made sense after all. An all-white peahen with all-black flesh. Maybe it made sense that the eye on a plucked feather split within a day; that the best rowers of her nation came not from the thorn of water but from the breath of its arid lands. Bereft of blue expanse, yet built with the right length, heft and wingspan. Perhaps there was no running on a stack of veils, she thought; it was up to the Lord to restore which version of exile.

She felt a nudge on her arm. The priestess was asking her to step forward and address the sea. After every storm they rode out together, and a different member of the neighbourhood was chosen for the act. In previous years, a man had walked to the water on his knees, murmuring 'Gange Gange', and another had thrown a puppet to the waves. A woman had danced around in furious circles wearing a thousand tiny diamond-shaped mirrors studded on her skirt and blouse. The wide water cresting to shatter twice and meet itself. Luni moved slowly ahead. Her daughter stayed with the old woman, having been given the responsibility of one of the puppies. She walked to where the sand got wet, then bent down and probed for a sweet spot. Once satisfied, from the little drawstring pouch she took out a sewing needle from a drawstring pouch that dangled down her wrist, raised it high, and, with one powerful stroke, stabbed the earth. The women gasped, the men averted their eyes. The priestess frowned at first, then smiled. The blood had shown elsewhere—a neat patch on Luni's behind.

# 36

HIMMO COMMENCED HER HUNT on the beach and found the fishermen assessing their boats for damage. The sea had given, as expected, and the shore was littered with tarp, tin, shell bits, a strewn deck of cards. She carefully moved past an ace face up, stepped flat-footed on the neck of a frosted bottle and saw a Lego worm. Her eyes combing the place, her hands plucking soles. Picked up a thin-striped flip-flop, then a leather one before suddenly pulling back. She had come upon a running shoe next to a pair of dirty dentures. Tender laces and next to it, on the other side, more than a little more than a sole: a piece of wall and a frog.

# 37

*TO THE LONESOME CROUCHING NUDE:*

*Belief is not enough; a belief brûléed*
*prompts that steep religion, brings home the new bone*
*catastrophe. The delicate face so singed*
*by the flames of towns and villages, of Noah himself.*
*Alas, upon the utmost bone, prayer no more.*
*Whose breath blooms the last souvenir and for whose solace?*
*Beware of the cows for there's a wolf in the hills, they say.*
*Then the lure of the blind teat.*
*'O all ye echo unwell—' Pluck her.*

*Rise now and stake the zipper.*

# 38

ARTH GENTLY SWAYED BACK AND forth as she sat on the fort's parapet. She had initially wanted to sit on the rocks by the sea but was reminded of the woman who would show up every now and then and place flowers on the boulders. She would sit a little while with a piece of paper in her hand. A crossword, Arth imagined. The way she'd rub her chin, look down at the paper, look up, some clue in her eyes. But Arth didn't want to attempt one herself, not after she'd learnt what the black blocks could do: they could make a swan. And a swan could make a saddle. Bumping into the woman risked getting involved, so Arth had returned to the safety of the cistern, prison and hospital, without the artist for the first time.

Her legs breathed the distance, but her insides sloshed around and into the void left open by the juggler's voice. One blue night soon after the storm, he was gone. A week later, Arth realized that the chalky ones were gone too. What was she to do now with this wicked absence? What if someone put something in there in the name of love? Staring out, she thought of the advice she'd got for keeping calm underwater: think happy thoughts. Maybe that could help close it up.

But she couldn't rely on those old images for they had a tendency to go wrong. One try and the girl on the plane is a plane herself, heading towards—

Arth shut her eyes. She slowed her breath and started searching.

What occurred first was an aviary but Arth found it empty. She started drifting again. Saw a boy swinging a shovel like a cricket bat. Why, it's only a foot or two of water, he said very sweetly, wearing whites he'd stitched on his own. Then he sat down and drew leaves on his clothes.

Arth shook her head. The shovel was relentless. *Arth*-dig-*Ardh*-dig-*Unarth*. The water struck was the asymmetry of a body, the very nature of language. Finding no recourse, she was considering heading back home when Arth heard a rustle behind her and turned to see a form brimming with light. Because of the sheer brightness, it did not declare itself instantly, and Arth had to take a few steps forward to see that it was a deer of some kind—a doe, a doe covered in bubbles. Had the spheres just been around the bulk of the creature's body, Arth could have imagined a life vest. But they were everywhere, and in all different sizes. A grape on the tip of the ear, a big bump on the rump. She moved closer to the glass globes but did not touch them. It was a spotted doe. Light spilling, seeping; bubbles within bubbles; distorted stone and sky. Arth's own strange reflection and the magnified beauty of the doe's body—every white and gold brushstroke on the immaculate skins of planets, the pitch-black eyes. *Bulbul-e*, Arth thought and smiled. At last, a bird had come, and that too this one of them all. And why wouldn't she have come, after the good hours Arth had spent in her childhood working old latches and squeaking across courts.

Look how pretty you are! Can I hang you from my tree?

She stepped back for a wider view. The dainty head was turned towards Arth, as though the creature had listened in a herd and pulled away from fallen fruit to regard the plainness of the civilized. Attentive, unafraid, inert with the power to recompense. Who had chosen that pose? Who had stretched the skin on the structure and gone through swatches to decide the precise colour of the eyeballs? Could be an experiment in grief, she thought. Perhaps a person or a group of people had perceived in the animal's dying not yet another roadkill nor some dazzling emptiness, but a woman, just an ordinary woman painting the word FONT in stark white.

And perhaps upon a closer look, they'd even glimpsed an R fading.

Arth wished her friend could have seen it. She'd call him home for dinner and tell him all about it. They could help Gul with the moulds and watch the sauce. She could bring up her mother's spoon collection; maybe make a quick Caesar. He could wear the cheese rings.

The doe's gaze went past Arth, farther away to where the sun inched closer to the water. Its slow yet eager descent towards no grand dimension of rest or appetite, but a humble hunger that devours the world and sustains it. Those slithering creatures whispering into old, sunk wood; digesting it and living there. Without a care about what in the name of God's mercy had once been loaded and lost or whose face was on the figurehead, the tunnelling masters of time, with wood in their stomachs and larvae under their gills, consumed it all. And what left for another day were ghosts of gilded glory and fragments torn and holey, beneath a placid surface that shivered only lightly for the soul without horror looking on, longing for a new song. Arth couldn't sing, but wanted to for her, and the wish alone was strong enough for the words to occur. Bestowed by the cistern, prison and hospital, adding a lift here and a little sway there, Arth offered a wreath of sound:

> whale that wallowed, whale that swallowed
> slow a greenhouse
> a lovely, blooming greenhouse
> look: cactus clocks clouds chrysanthemums
> pelvis purple pansies poses
> rubber robins ribbons roses
> look: scribbled starlight of Scheherazade
> look: here, my braided faith
> look: here, our tiny hands
> look: here, here, here

And she heard, and she came, the one who'd left as wild as a losing stream. With her white train lapping and her soft quills, she slipped close and curled a finger around Arth's. Then what was said was almost a whisper.

The first subjunctive the guests gave us and I stood up to dance with you. We danced all night, remember? We danced. Oh we danced.

—

The line owes like the lip of a clutch. Oh how the stark night longs to shut it.

# The author's prayer for the book

*My dear poor sweet little snowman*
*Can a prayer be so complete?*
*Carpathia in sleep*
*can taste herself.*

RESPONSE:

AS_ENT AS_ENT

# Notes

The dialogue *saala ret ka jaanwar yahan samandar mein kaiko marne aaya* is from the 1992 Hindi film *Dharavi*.

The cyclone shelter's draped exterior draws from the Kuakata shelter built by architect Kashef Mahboob Chowdhury in Bangladesh.

The details of the ship *Jhelum* were drawn from the article 'The hulk *Jhelum*: a derivative expression of late British Indiaman ship-building', *International Journal of Nautical Archaeology and Underwater Exploration* (Mensun Bound, 1990).

'Sunset burn little burn' is a translation of *Yuyake Koyake*, a children's song played every evening across the Minato area of Tokyo to test the early warning systems in preparation for a big earthquake.

The song fragment *Baby but the whales don't fall like snow* takes from the article titled 'Whales Don't Fall Like Snow: Reply to Jermet', *Conservation Biology* (Butman, Carlton and Palumbi, April 1996).

Bugs Bunny's dialogues take from and are inspired by the 1950 cartoon film *What's Up Doc?*

The line 'Call me how tell tonight' bows to Agha Shahid Ali's poem 'Tonight'.

The ritual of placing a stool, a comb and a tiny mirror outside homes is practised in Assam in anticipation of *Bordoisila*, the wild wind that marks the beginning of monsoon.

Copycat's section on forgiveness draws from Catherine Denardo's moving feature 'The Lonely Orca', *Nautlius Magazine*, April 2023.

Sangai is an endemic species of Eld's deer inhabiting Keibul Lamjao National Park in Manipur.

The fragment *Jaiyega nahin, mera tamasha khatam nahin hua, joker ka tamasha khatam nahin hua, jaiyega nahin, jaiyega nahin* is from the song 'Jeena Yahan

Marna Yahan', featured in the 1970 Hindi movie *Mera Naam Joker.*

The chant *tuki tuki papa* was formed from the native names of the whale shark in the Philippines (*tuki*) and Kenya (*papa shillingi*).

The story of the ruler's death concealed with decaying dolphins evolved from an account of the demise of Chinese emperor Qin Shi Huang in 210 BCE.

The line 'Nerik gave birth to something resembling the eggs of a sea turtle and Flora gave birth to something like intestines' is from Kathy Jetñil-Kijiner's poem 'Monster' quoting from *The Sociocultural Impact of Nuclear Weapons Tests in the Marshall Islands* by Glenn Alcalay (unpublished field report: 1981), 1–2.

Mentions of lost and coming earthquakes were formed after reading accounts and sections of *The Gospel of Matthew,* Chapter 27*; The Ramayana*; eight lines discovered by seismologist Paolo Galli in a Hebrew prayer book from 1446; and *Quran* (99: 6–8) translated by Marmaduke Pickthall.

The maths problem about two students contributing to earthquake relief funds was found on the website *Toppr*, a leading ed-tech platform in India.

The 'Did You Feel It' questionnaire is a composite of surveys posted by the United States Geological Survey and the National Centre of Seismology, Government of India.

The doe adorned with glass bubbles stepped into the writing after an encounter with artist Kohei Nawa's *PixCell-Deer#24*.

# Acknowledgements

I am thankful to my sister Pallavi, who, despite being a younger sibling, guides, protects and judges like an older one. Thank you for storing the scraps when there was nothing but the hand's insistence for the word.

To Indra, for his patience and generous supply of laughter and watermelons. I hope you can count on me as much as I count on you.

To Richard, Krissy, Grace, Molly, Andrada, Anil, Bethany, Tony, John, Eva and Thiago: I am so glad I found you in Boston. Thank you for your friendship.

To Soumya, whose kindness nurtures our shared love of the craft. Thank you.

I will never forget those who held on tight during the pandemic: my family, Richard, Molly, Andrada, Anil, Indra, Srishti, Steffi, Ann. I am deeply grateful.

To Anthony Edgar, your faith in me since I was a teenager has been extraordinary. Thank you.

To Vineet Gahalaut, who lives and breathes geology. Thank you for teaching me and sharing your beautiful mind.

To all my gurus—humans and other beings—who, in this passage of life, have blessed the joker and the journalist. Thank you.

To Santoshi Didi, Neelam Didi and Dayanand Bhaiya, whose care and forgiveness make me possible. I have done little to deserve you, but I am deeply grateful.

It has been an absolute pleasure to work with my captain and editor Isha Banerji, whose gentle support through the drafts made me a better writer. And to Teesta Guha Sarkar, Udyotna Kumar, Amit Malhotra and the entire team at Pan Macmillan India, for their dedication to every aspect of the book.

To my lovely agent Kate Evans, for always encouraging my experiments. Thank you for taking this journey with me.

To the writers and artists whose work supported me through the making of this text: Anne Carson, Agha Shahid Ali, Bhanu Kapil, Christine Sun Kim, Clarice

Lispector, John Milton, Jorie Graham, Lisa Robertson, Primo Levi, Roland Barthes, T. S. Eliot and my guide Toni Morrison. Please accept this book as a humble offering.

Above all, to my maa and papa. I love you. You bleed into this flood and anoint it.